S0-AAB-560

THE
MUMMY

THE
MUMMY
TOMB OF THE DRAGON EMPEROR

A novel by
Max Allan Collins

Based on the screenplay by
Alfred Gough and Miles Millar

BERKLEY BOULEVARD BOOKS, NEW YORK

THE BERKLEY PUBLISHING GROUP
Published by the Penguin Group
Penguin Group (USA) Inc.
375 Hudson Street, New York, New York 10014, USA
Penguin Group (Canada), 90 Eglinton Avenue East, Suite 700, Toronto, Ontario M4P 2Y3, Canada
(a division of Pearson Penguin Canada Inc.)
Penguin Books Ltd., 80 Strand, London WC2R 0RL, England
Penguin Group Ireland, 25 St. Stephen's Green, Dublin 2, Ireland (a division of Penguin Books Ltd.)
Penguin Group (Australia), 250 Camberwell Road, Camberwell, Victoria 3124, Australia
(a division of Pearson Australia Group Pty. Ltd.)
Penguin Books India Pvt. Ltd., 11 Community Centre, Panchsheel Park, New Delhi—110 017, India
Penguin Group (NZ), 67 Apollo Drive, Rosedale, North Shore 0632, New Zealand
(a division of Pearson New Zealand Ltd.)
Penguin Books (South Africa) (Pty.) Ltd., 24 Sturdee Avenue, Rosebank, Johannesburg 2196,
South Africa

Penguin Books Ltd., Registered Offices: 80 Strand, London WC2R 0RL, England

This is a work of fiction. Names, characters, places, and incidents either are the product of the author's imagination or are used fictitiously, and any resemblance to actual persons, living or dead, business establishments, events, or locales is entirely coincidental. The publisher does not have any control over and does not assume any responsibility for author or third-party websites or their content.

THE MUMMY: TOMB OF THE DRAGON EMPEROR

A Berkley Boulevard Book / published by arrangement with Universal Studios Licensing LLLP

PRINTING HISTORY
Berkley Boulevard mass-market movie tie-in edition / July 2008

Copyright © 2008 Universal Studios Licensing LLLP
Book design by Tiffany Estreicher

Mummy: Tomb of the Dragon Emperor is a trademark and copyright of Universal Studios.

All rights reserved.
No part of this book may be reproduced, scanned, or distributed in any printed or electronic form without permission. Please do not participate in or encourage piracy of copyrighted materials in violation of the author's rights. Purchase only authorized editions.
For information, address: The Berkley Publishing Group,
a division of Penguin Group (USA) Inc.,
375 Hudson Street, New York, New York 10014.

ISBN: 978-0-425-22313-0

BERKLEY BOULEVARD®
Berkley Boulevard Books are published by The Berkley Publishing Group,
a division of Penguin Group (USA) Inc.,
375 Hudson Street, New York, New York 10014.
BERKLEY BOULEVARD® is a registered trademark of Penguin Group (USA) Inc.
The BERKLEY BOULEVARD logo is a trademark belonging to Penguin Group (USA) Inc.

PRINTED IN THE UNITED STATES OF AMERICA

10   9   8   7   6   5   4   3   2   1

If you purchased this book without a cover, you should be aware that this book is stolen property. It was reported as "unsold and destroyed" to the publisher, and neither the author nor the publisher has received any payment for this "stripped book."

*"People make mistakes in life
through believing too much,
but they have a damned dull time
if they believe too little."*

—James Hilton

"Study the past if you would define the future."

—Confucius

"Eat, drink and be merry for tomorrow we die."

—Imhotep

·❮ PROLOGUE ❯·

Emperor of Evil

EDITOR'S NOTE: The following draws heavily upon the work Tomb of the Dragon Emperor: Myth and Mystery *(Bembridge Press, London, 1948) by Dr. Evelyn O'Connell. Among the many accomplishments of Dr. O'Connell, whose doctorate was in the library sciences, were significant contributions to the fields of archaeology and Egyptology. The daughter of noted Egyptologist Howard Carnahan, one of the discoverers in 1922 of the tomb of Tutankhamen, Dr. O'Connell was curator of the Cairo Museum (1925 to 1927) and in her later years held, at various times, the same post at the British Museum in London. In between she wrote a number of well-respected academic works as well as several popular novels that drew upon her experiences on digs and in the field with her well-known husband, explorer Richard O'Connell. The O'Connells raised a son, Alex, who shared his parents' enthusiasm for antiquities and has followed in the famous footsteps of his parents.*

Long ago, in a time of darkness two hundred years before the birth of Christ, China suffered under the rule of a ruthless emperor—Er Shi Huangdi of the Qin Dynasty. The Emperor's thirst for power seemed unquenchable, and his willingness to brutally, mercilessly dispatch his foes earned fear for his army throughout the ancient world.

After vanquishing the barbarians of the north, Emperor Er Shi Huangdi's army formed a huge encampment among the towering Chinese pyramids of Ningxia, a desertlike region bordering Shaanxi and Gansu. At dusk of the day of their latest great battle, the warriors rested, smells of food cooked over campfires wafting through the peaceful tent city, hearty laughter and drink-fueled braggadocio punctuating the calm.

Now and then more abrasive sounds threatened the after-battle lull, in particular a line of barbarian captives held in neck stocks and chains and moving along at the request of sharp whipcracks. Thundering past them, an armored messenger on horseback headed toward the enormous black tent whose banners were emblazoned with a three-headed dragon; here the messenger dismounted at a gallop to approach the Emperor's sentries.

Within the expansive tent could be found fittings as grand as those of any palace, a black-and-gold interior whose masculine richness was enhanced by the flickering candlelight of wooden chandeliers. Here, in black armor adorned with intricately carved jade and finely molded gold, stood the Emperor, a figure as stoic as a statue, and with angular features just as finely sculpted. Er Shi Huangdi's eyes, dark and penetrating in the pale oval mask of his face, explored the architectural model displayed on a sprawling table that also included engineering plans of what would one day be known as the Great Wall of China.

With him, but paying him the respect of distance, were General Ming Guo—tall and somber, his dark-eyed demeanor rivaling his emperor's—and Li Zhou, the boyish, athletic-looking chief eunuch, who despite his youth wore the gold-and-jade medallion of head minister. All were dressed in black, as were the attendants on the periphery numbering twenty much-less-important eunuchs and assorted palace guards.

When the sentries allowed him entry, the messenger approached not the Emperor but Li Zhou, presenting the scroll to the head minister, who broke the seal and gave what seemed a cursory glance at the Chinese text before passing the message to the Emperor.

Quickly, Er Shi Huangdi gleaned its contents. Then

his eyes raised to those of his head minister and they traded smiles so slight, so brief, that even the nearby General Ming Guo did not catch the exchange.

Looking at no one, speaking to everyone, the Emperor said, "Leave me."

Bows of respect were paid, and the Emperor's demand heeded, while Er Shi Huangdi himself continued to study the model of the wall he would build, and the map of the lands he would one day rule. Those nearest the Emperor knew that he might stand for hours in quiet, intense contemplation of the plans, the future, that the three-dimensional map suggested.

The night that followed was clear and crisp with stars that seemed like punctures in the blackness of the sky, letting in pinholes of light from the heavens on the other side. The camp soon settled into near quiet, disrupted only by a few drunken songs from the happy, exhausted warriors, none of whom had the slightest notion that the invaders were about to be invaded.

Men dressed in black in this camp were no rarity, but these two men in black did not belong here. As they crept across the slumbering encampment, they went unseen until nearing the Emperor's grand tent, where a sentry caught their movement and was about to call out a query when a third man in black used one hand to slip a knife in the sentry's back, and another to come around and cover the man's mouth, turning a cry into a muffled gasp. Then the sentry slipped to the ground, sounding no alarm, forever silent.

Within the elaborate world of his palacelike tent, the Emperor slept on a surprisingly unpretentious pallet, a soldier-like berth for so powerful a man. He seemed deep asleep and wholly unaware as a blade slit the tent and made an entrance for the trio of assassins, who slipped in low and quick, daggers in hand, already poised to strike.

The Emperor, at rest, had lost his charismatic presence and seemed almost small, an easy target, a helpless victim. As one assassin took position at the head of the simple bed, behind the intended victim, with the other two assassins on either side of the bed, Er Shi Huangdi might well have been a slumbering youth.

But he was not.

And what happened next defied the senses of the men who had come to kill him.

The Emperor's eyes snapped open as from under the sheets emerged a sword, which he tossed to his left hand, quickly filling his right with a gold dragon-hilt dagger, which he plunged in a backward stab deep into the chest of the assassin behind him. At the same time, the assassin on the Emperor's left bedside, lunging in with his own dagger ready to strike, had been pierced by his intended victim's sudden sword-in-hand. A second blade struck the already dying assassin in the back, as his compatriot across the bed

5

accidentally stabbed his slumped comrade. Er Shi Huangdi had already vacated the bed, rolling off nimbly, dragon dagger still in hand.

All this happened in about two seconds, and to the surviving assassin's credit, his reaction was to charge across the bed and the corpse on it, to dive toward Er Shi Huangdi, who met the motion of the assassin's downward dagger with the hilt of his own, and used the momentum—and a helping hand—to flip the would-be killer up and over his head. But the assassin landed on his feet, catlike, and sprang at once into action.

So did the Emperor.

The close-quarters duel with daggers produced sharp clangs that made a frantic, dissonant music as these two skilled warriors met in a knife fight for the ages. Shadows on the tent walls under the flickering candlelight reflected actions so swift and deft, the most skilled dancers and acrobats would have bowed in deference.

But this tough young assassin, his forehead scarred with his cult's brand, was no match for the Emperor, who cut the man's wrist, leaving a deep searing slash, popping fingers open and sending the intruder's dagger flying.

Now, for the first time, the disarmed assassin flinched and the Emperor spun and kicked and sat his opponent down rudely in a chair. Within a moment, Er Shi Huangdi held his dagger's tip to the visitor's sternum.

The commotion finally brought in a frowning, concerned, if sleep-frazzled General Ming Guo, sword drawn, followed by a strangely serene Li Zhou and a coterie of eunuch guards.

To his seated foe, the Emperor—pressing the tip of the dagger into the man's flesh—demanded, "Who sent you, dog? Tell me and I may yet let you live."

The assassin swallowed. "The Governor . . . the Governor of Chu."

And now the Emperor smiled and his eyes turned strangely languid. "Good," he murmured. "Good."

Ming Guo, not following, glanced in confusion at Head Minister Li Zhou, who merely stood with folded arms and a faintly smiling countenance.

The Emperor withdrew the threat of the dagger point, then stepped away, turning his back to his prisoner as he said, "I bring peace and order to the land . . . and this is how my people repay me?"

From a sleeve, the assassin flicked a knife and, with this new weapon in his hand, launched himself at the Emperor . . .

. . . who, almost casually, without looking, backhanded his dragon dagger into the attacking man's heart, not even bothering to turn and see his opponent gasp and crumple into a pile of dying flesh.

Ming Guo, distraught, dropped to his knees before his Emperor. "I have failed you, my lord!"

"No."

"But I have!"

"No, my good and faithful servant." The Emperor's smile now was serenely benign. "I was well aware of this plot. I was prepared to welcome my guests."

Ming Guo frowned up at Er Shi Huangdi. "You *knew*? And yet you said nothing? You allowed it to go on?"

The Emperor's smile turned wry as his eyes met those of his head minister. But his words were for his general: "I wanted a war . . . and now I have one."

Ming Guo, still on his knees, seemed to catch up, all at once. He nodded. "Yes, my lord. No one can deny you the right of retaliation."

"Dawn will be here soon," Er Shi Huangdi said. He was already heading out of the palacelike tent. "Get on your feet, my friend. We will ride for Chu."

Over the weeks and months ahead, the Emperor used the provocation of his attempted assassination to launch what would become a reign of terror and destruction.

In his tent, on the table given over to the terracotta map, the Emperor would move small clay figurines of war, game pieces representing his vast army before whom lay the rest of China. Then on the battlefield, he would lead the flesh-and-blood versions of those terra-cotta toy soldiers in a life-and-death game of conquest.

What was a cold game in the planning became a hellish reality to the vanquished—when the capital city of Chu burned, citizens scattered and ran, hoping to avoid the Emperor's soldiers, who routinely arrested the men, separating them from their women and children. No province was spared as the army of Er Shi Huangdi rolled across the land, raping, pillaging, an unstoppable, merciless killing machine.

No one in the inner circle dared challenge the warrior Emperor, though secretly his general, Ming Guo, felt no pride in these brutal endeavors. The valiant general had not helped defeat barbarian hordes in order to become a barbarian himself. He would watch with hidden disgust and secret shame as the Emperor, astride a black stallion, personally supervised executions, as if the deaths of these poor unimportant souls were necessary to feed the flames of Er Shi Huangdi's burning ambition.

And as the fires of their scorched cities fought the night, long lines of prisoners in neck stocks would be marched in, past the Emperor, who watched on prancing horseback, and then lined up ten at a time to kneel at chopping blocks. The executioners would raise axes above the necks of the captives and, at the Emperor's signal, would swing the blades savagely down—an all-too-familiar crunch followed by the thump of blade meeting wood echoing in the night . . . and in Ming Guo's conscience.

The general knew that the Emperor would not stop until he ruled all under heaven, and yet the great ruler seemed somehow childlike as he moved the terra-cotta game pieces on the big table in his tent. Now the clay soldiers had been moved north and south from the Himalayas to the China Sea.

The Emperor enslaved his vanquished enemies and forced them to build his great wall, soldiers in armor supervising workers in rags. Breaking rocks, shoveling dirt into pits, ramming the earth, laying bricks, swinging massive granite blocks into place, these warriors-turned-slaves endured months of brutal work, spurred by the spears of their supervisors. Their reward would be rides in carts to quarries where—when it was time for the Emperor to move on to the next construction site—the exhausted slaves would be dumped screaming into pits. Such workers would build a section of the Emperor's great wall, and then be buried beneath it—no need to transport slave labor when more slave labor awaited.

The job was as ambitious as it was grandiose, but soon the Great Wall of China stretched as far as the eye could see, its ramparts patrolled by the Emperor's armored, spear-wielding warriors, their bravery in battle replaced by cruelty to their captives. The remarkable feat took twenty years, and the final tribute to the historic effort—and the godlike man behind it—was the construction of a mammoth stone bust of the Emperor in warrior garb atop a turreted temple devoted not to any deity, but to Er Shi Huangdi himself.

The severe, accurate likeness, up a massive flight of stone stairs, seemed to survey the Emperor's domain, not just the Great Wall but the sprawling capital city nearby. Broad, tree-lined thoroughfares all led to the same place: the palace, a formidable structure that seemed more fortress than royal dwelling, which was perhaps fitting, as Er Shi Huangdi was no benign potentate, rather a brutal dictator, a reality his people had long since accepted but which still compelled his trusted general, Ming Guo, to live in private shame.

A ramp from the Great Wall led to an area where the Emperor's golden chariot and its steeds were being attended by slaves and palace guards outside a stone temple. In the subterranean chamber below not just the temple but the Great Wall itself, the Emperor dutifully studied the dark arts with the help of five mystics, each of whom represented one of the five elements—fire, water, earth, wood and metal.

The Emperor's mystics taught him well. In much less time than the Great Wall had taken, Er Shi Huangdi had attained an impressive mastery of those five elements. The dark underground chamber that served as the Emperor's school had at one end a waterwheel and an enormous clockwork astrolabe—an astronomical instrument used to study the position of the stars and sun. The domed ceiling was a grotesque bas-relief consisting of corpses of enemies of the Emperor, vanquished warriors condemned to eternally support the Great Wall above.

Older now, his still-youthful face cut by an elegant goatee, his lithe form again in black jade-encrusted armor, Er Shi Huangdi walked down a fire-bordered pathway to ascend a stairway to the Altar of the Five Elements, around which stood the mystics who schooled him in the manipulation of the physical world. Below, on the periphery of the chamber, were head minister Li Zhou and a small coterie of eunuch priests, heads bowed.

The Emperor moved to the circular altar at which were stations representing and containing (in bowl-like recessions on its surface) each element. Nearest him, one such recession swirled with fire . . .

. . . and into this, the Emperor dipped his palms to bring back blazing handfuls of flame, which he began to mold, his flesh unscathed, as if the licking yellow-and-blue tongues were harmless, and to him they were. He fashioned a burning ball, bounced it in one hand, then with a nod raised water from its receptacle to encircle, and enshroud, the flames he held without quenching them; and when water turned to steam, his gesture turned it to ice.

And now, within that ball of ice, flames danced, as the watching mystics solemnly smiled, pleased with their pupil.

Er Shi Huangdi, who sought ever-more-powerful ways to satisfy his own longing for complete control of everything and everyone, also smiled; but not in the enigmatic, wise way of his teachers—more like a child with a new toy.

"I will use my dark powers," he said, "to curse the

souls of my enemies. Let them hold up my Great Wall for all eternity!"

And again the mystics smiled, and nodded with respect and admiration and pride.

Later, in the palace, the Emperor studied the table with its terra-cotta map—and terra-cotta warriors—that had accompanied him across thousands of miles through hundreds of battles, its arrangement now reflecting all that he had achieved. The three-dimensional map, on a table expanded now to twenty feet by twenty feet, was lined with a network of roads and canals connecting new cities throughout all of China, garrisoned with his clay-soldier army.

And yet beyond China, past his Great Wall, lay uncharted territory—other lands remaining to be conquered.

Er Shi Huangdi realized that all his grand ambitions could not be achieved in one lifetime. One enemy remained to be defeated, the most powerful enemy of all.

Death itself.

The Emperor reached throughout his kingdom for anyone who might know of a sorcerer privy to arts even darker than those of Er Shi Huangdi's own mystics. A slave stepped forward with news of one such wizard in a distant province, and was rewarded with a quick death, which was as close as Er Shi Huangdi came to mercy.

With his personal guard of twelve, Ming Guo—still the Emperor's most trusted general—rode through the palace gates, setting out to find this wizard. After months of riding, the journey ended at a rugged escarpment and a looming complex of buildings, some wood, some stone. The central and most impressive of these—though not the largest structure—was a templelike affair straddling a narrow gorge. The only access was a narrow staircase carved from the rock of the steep slope.

Leaving his soldiers behind, Ming Guo made the climb.

Soon the general was stepping cautiously into a cramped chamber dwarfed by its own massive wooden beams, which were part of the structural design that allowed it to straddle the gorge. He found himself in what was clearly an ancient apothecary.

In the dimly lighted gloom, on the stone floor, were smoking vats and billowing vials; all around were shelves rife with boxes and jars of mysterious ingredients, and urns everywhere, with some vessels hanging by twine from the inverted V of the ceiling. Smells were acrid here, sweet there, and unfamiliar everywhere.

Down at the far end of the chamber, Ming Guo could make out a figure; but it was not that of a wizard. This was, perhaps, the wizard's assistant, a striking woman with high cheekbones and large, dark eyes, in a purple robe that, while faded, was no less beautiful. Her long dark hair curved around her angular, intelligent face to spill down over one shoulder. Her form was slender yet shapely enough that the robe could not hide all of her charms.

She looked up sharply yet casually as she ground a pestle into a small mortar, obviously at work on some potion or other. "We do not often have visitors from Qin province."

As he crossed the room, sidestepping jars and pots, Ming Guo asked, "Who has told you I am from Qin province?"

Her smile was faint and, it seemed to Ming Guo at least, ethereal. "*You* have. Just now. You are a soldier? A general?"

"I am." He was at the base of the small platform on which her preparation table rested. He looked up at her; she looked down at him.

"You are surprised that I am a woman."

"Perhaps. But not all surprises are unpleasant."

She smiled again but her eyes returned to her work. "You seek my father."

"I do, if your father is the great wizard whose skills have reached the ears of the Emperor."

She said nothing, working the pestle into the mortar. Then: "My father died some years ago. I, Zi Yuan, have taken up his mantle."

"He had no sons?"

"No. Just an unworthy daughter."

Unworthy or not, the wizard's daughter already had Ming Guo under her spell, though no magic had been involved other than the chemistry that can pass between a man and woman in one electric moment.

"My emperor seeks to extend his life," Ming Guo said, "beyond that of the normal confines of human existence."

Zi Yuan raised an eyebrow as she watched her work. "That is beyond my powers," she admitted. "That would have been beyond even my father's powers."

Ming Guo bowed. "I regret to hear this." Then his eyes raised to hers. "I would have enjoyed the journey back to Qin province with you as my travelling companion."

Again she smiled and something pleasantly wicked came into it. "Well . . . perhaps I *could* help your emperor. . . ."

And two months later, in the throne room of the fortresslike palace, Ming Guo presented Zi Yuan to Er Shi Huangdi.

"Wizards are men," the Emperor said as he lifted her chin with his finger, clearly struck by her radiance, "but you are not a man. And yet . . . I am not disappointed."

"Thank you, my lord."

"Has my trusted general shared with you my problem? My ambitions outdistance a normal life span. Can you be of help?"

Standing before him with head lowered, she said, "I do not possess the answer you seek, my lord."

His forehead tightened. "Then you have disappointed me, after all."

Her eyes met his. "I *do* know where an answer *might* be found."

"Good. Good. Then I bid you find it."

She bowed again. "Yes, my lord."

As she exited, escorted by eunuch guards, the Emperor gestured for Ming Guo to lean near.

"No man is to touch her," the Emperor said. "She is mine."

Ming Guo responded with a nod that was also a bow. The Emperor could not know that his trusted general had long since disobeyed that order.

Still, the Emperor may have had his doubts. Over the months to come, Ming Guo and Zi Yuan were not aware that the Emperor's head minister traveled discreetly behind them. They were blissfully ignorant of Li Zhou's presence as they rode away from the capital city across a sea of golden sand dunes. They remained unmindful of this shadow even as they approached the Monastery of Turfan on the Silk Road, kicking up clouds of dust as their horses raced toward the gates of the enormous minaret, an architectural wonder that mingled Chinese and Islamic traditions.

The lovely, enigmatic Zi Yuan spent her days searching the library for ancient texts, often seated at the circular desk in the midst of the colossal library chamber, poring over scrolls unearthed from long-forgotten boxes and bins.

Hour upon fruitless hour, the wizard's daughter worked, until finally—at the bottom of yet another documents container—she came upon a dusty puzzle box. This she recognized as a kind of key, and she was able to quickly flower it open, its petals indeed comprising a shape that she felt would fit a slot on a large lacquer tube she had examined days before. Though that tube had been replete with arcane warnings, she stepped unhesitatingly to the shelf and inserted and turned the oversized key, setting forth a chain reaction of unlocking mechanisms.

Startled momentarily, she quickly opened the tube to withdraw a bizarre timeworn object that appeared to be a sort of scroll, fashioned from human bones no less, and onto which Chinese letters had been etched. These she recognized at once as the fabled Oracle Bones, a collection of medical and mystical knowledge from the mists of antiquity.

In her bedchamber at the monastery, Zi Yuan shared this discovery with Ming Guo, as they lay naked in each other's arms. . . .

Unfortunately, another discovery was made by the Emperor's man, Li Zhou, who had been watching the lovers through a peephole, confirming long-held suspicions. Ming Guo and Zi Yuan had thought they could keep their passion a secret, but they should have known: an Emperor like Er Shi Huangdi has eyes everywhere.

Fate did grant the couple one favor: while in his lover's embrace in the darkened bedchamber, Ming Guo spied a flicker of light indicating they were indeed being spied upon. The naked Ming Guo raced to a door that opened onto the library, where he could see the fleeing figure of the eunuch who was his emperor's head minister. The general turned in dismay to the beautiful daughter of a wizard, and they shared looks of dread, their forbidden love discovered.

"We should flee, my love," she told him as they embraced on the bed.

"There is nowhere to hide," Ming Guo said. "Nor can my love for you erase my duty as a soldier. I may disapprove of things my emperor does, but I must stay loyal, or I am nothing."

"Your loyalty should be to our love."

"And it is. Only by returning, and throwing myself upon . . ." He could barely say it. ". . . the mercy of my lord may we be spared."

But though he spoke the word *we*, Ming Guo knew his best, his only hope, would be that Zi Yuan herself might be spared. His doom had been sealed when that eunuch had seen him in Zi Yuan's bed.

A hot, dusty morning marked the return of the two riders through the palace gates. They rode slowly, heads held high, through row upon row of warriors assembled in the palace courtyard. The two rode to the foot of the steps of the palace, dismounted, and then the lovers bowed to each other.

Softly, her eyes moist, Zi Yuan said, "Good-bye, my love."

"Not good-bye," Ming Guo said. "For whatever happens, our love will live on. That much we know. And I would face far worse than Er Shi Huangdi to have shared this time with you."

Zi Yuan nodded solemnly, then turned and began the climb, as the rest of this journey was hers to make.

In the throne room, she found herself alone with the Emperor, at whose feet she knelt, withdrawing from her robe the Oracle Bones. She held the object up to him. "Your answer is here, my lord."

He did not take the unusual scroll, but said, "You have served me well. In return, I will grant you anything."

She looked up from her kneeling posture. "*Anything*, my lord?"

"Anything you desire, yes."

Zi Yuan swallowed. She did not stand. Her eyes sought some sign in his blank expression, but none presented itself.

Finally she said, "I have only one wish, my lord. And I mean you no disrespect. But I wish to spend the rest of my days with Ming Guo."

"Of course," he said, his voice, his manner, as calm as a summer day. "Just read."

She rose and unrolled the scroll and began to read in ancient Sanskrit.

"Stop!" His brow tightened in suspicion. "What is this strange language?"

"It is more ancient than the Shan, from a land at the end of the world."

". . . Read on."

What Zi Yuan did not say was that this was a dialect so ancient only a sorcerer or a sorcerer's daughter might know it.

And what she read was this: *"In the dark heart of the creator, from the depths of hate, from the mud of evil, should Er Shi Huangdi betray my love and me, cover this man with the dirt of his soul. Bake him in the kiln of torture and enshroud him in a tomb of clay for all eternity."*

The Emperor's suspicion had faded—this was, after all, a spell, and Er Shi Huangdi did not need to understand the words for them to do their work. He felt a tingling, a warmth, a rush he had never before sensed, coursing through him.

From the window across the chamber came the whinnying of horses in the courtyard below, a terrified nickering that belied the Emperor's calm manner. Unsettling though the sounds were, Zi Yuan continued to read aloud in the tongue of antiquity . . .

. . . *unaware that the animals were reacting, as soldiers bound the hands and feet of Ming Guo, other soldiers looking on, as fearful as the nostril-flaring horses, sickened at the sight of their beloved general being prepared for the worst of deaths.*

A wind kicked up dust and blew through palace windows to whip brazier fires and further give lie to the Emperor's peaceful demeanor.

Finally, Zi Yuan closed the scroll. "It is done."

Eyes glittering, fists raised, the Emperor breathed in deep. "Your words were a mystery to me, but I feel their strength coursing through my veins. It is working. I can *feel* it."

"Eternal life is yours, my lord. You have received a great gift. And you have bestowed a great gift upon me. I am grateful."

He gestured to the wizard's daughter. "Come. Come to the window."

Er Shi Huangdi walked her to the window and revealed to her a sight that filled Zi Yuan with horror. Down in the courtyard, Ming Guo was tethered between four teams of horses. The eyes of the lovers met in desperation.

The Emperor gestured down to his general, and the horses who threatened to tear him apart. He spoke loud enough for all to hear: "Become my queen and I will forgive this traitor. I will let him live!"

The Emperor's voice had not stopped echoing across the courtyard when Ming Guo shouted, *"Don't believe him!"*

22

Defiant, she turned to the Emperor. "He is right. You will never keep your word."

"You are wise," Er Shi Huangdi admitted, and with a smirk he gave the signal.

The teams of horses took off in four directions and the Emperor watched with pleasure as his former general was torn asunder, ripped into pieces that trailed the steeds, limbs bouncing along grotesquely, leaving streaks of blood in the dust.

Zi Yuan, who had turned away from the atrocity, not wanting its sight in her memory, now found herself in the foul embrace of the man who had just ordered her lover's gruesome demise.

"Now join Ming Guo in hell," Er Shi Huangdi said.

She felt the blade pierce her side and she staggered back a step and looked down with wide eyes at the dagger plunged to its dragon hilt, just under ribs and above the hipbone. He withdrew the blade and flung it to the floor, his upper lip curling in contempt.

But as the wizard's child fell to her knees, the Emperor felt within him a terrible, strange shifting. This was a pain the likes of which he'd never experienced. He had been wounded in battle and healed; he had suffered sickness and survived. But this was a molten churning that filled his very veins, coursed through his every organ, with fiery agony. Tears slipped from his eyes, and he wiped them away only to see that they were brown—like liquid clay!

He stared in shock at the kneeling, bleeding woman. "What have you *done* to me, witch? What spell did you cast in that ancient tongue?"

She smiled up at him, and now her upper lip peeled back in disgust, and triumph. "I have cursed you! You, and all those who spill blood in your name."

From his temples and his forehead, a brown slurry cascaded like thick, ugly perspiration, streaming down his face. Screaming, he tried to wipe it off, but still it came, gushing now. He tore at his robe only to find the muddy substance now oozing from his armpits. And from under his topknot, a fountain of gooey mud erupted like lava, flowing down his body, soaking his robes and his boots.

Zi Yuan got to her feet and moved away, not dying, but her wound serious indeed. Li Zhou and the imperial guards, spears in hand, rushed in, only to back away in horror. Neither the guards nor the head minister even noticed as the wizard's daughter slipped away in the shadows.

And yet the process of Zi Yuan's terra-cotta curse had only begun: *now came the fire.*

Five hundred times hotter than the flames that had consumed so many cities during Er Shi Huangdi's reign of conquest, a white heat ignited, its aura glowing as the flames consumed the Emperor and baked the man alive. For a time he screamed, his howls those of a man suffering as no man ever had before, his eye-

24

balls cooking white as the clay fired, his shrill dismay echoing. . . .

The screams summoned the Emperor's army, but as they formed up in rows to secure the palace, they began to weep their own muddy tears. Soon they too were emitting bloodcurdling wails, as the stunned soldiers looked at one another in fear and surprise as the oozing mud came from within to consume them from without.

Their master was a step ahead of them, his terra-cotta shell almost fired hard by now. The great ruler could barely move, staggering helplessly as his agony continued. The imperial guard, dumbfounded by what they'd witnessed, did not try to stop Zi Yuan as she left the palace. They were too busy watching as the terrible aura of heat finally ceased and revealed the smoking statue that the Emperor, now encased in a ceramic skin, had become. This reddish-brown shell he would wear for millennia, but Zi Yuan had not lied in her promise of eternal life: he would indeed remain alive within his terra-cotta cocoon . . . but in suspended animation. . . .

In the courtyard, hunching in pain, Zi Yuan cantered her horse as she rode out, through a motionless army that had shared its master's fate, smoke rising lazily from their terra-cotta forms. So it was that the wizard's daughter rode off into the night, never to be seen again . . . or at least never in recorded history.

As for the Emperor, Er Shi Huangdi was buried by

his eunuchs, who had been spared this hellish fate, his terra-cotta warriors interred with him.

Here the chapter of the evil Emperor would seem at an end. But in ancient texts it is written that should Er Shi Huangdi ever be freed from his terra-cotta prison, he will again become a force of evil, only on a scale to make his previous savagery pale . . . raising his warriors to lay siege to the entire world—a shape-shifting master of the five elements, and a slave to his undying thirst for conquest.

·❦ 1 ❧·

Call to Adventure

Oxfordshire, England

With steely-eyed, life-or-death determination, Rick O'Connell stared at his foe.

"You can run," he said, his voice softly menacing, "but you can't hide."

Among the enemies Richard O'Connell had stared down in his time were Tuaregs on horseback in the Sahara, in his French Foreign Legion days, and any number of bloodthirsty mercenaries who'd attempted to steal the treasures he and his Egyptologist wife had uncovered for museums on various digs. And this did not touch upon the assorted reanimated mummies he'd dispatched, from pygmies to high priests to the great Imhotep himself, and then there were the Med-jai warriors, and of course the Scorpion King, and . . .

. . . the fat brown trout swimming lazily, arrogantly through the warm, gently flowing waters of a chalk stream theoretically perfect for fly-fishing.

On this beautiful spring afternoon in 1946, O'Connell—Rick to some, "Ricochet" Rick to others—was wielding neither rifle nor machine gun, and certainly not a golden spear opened out of the Scepter of Osiris. A few years past forty, O'Connell retained the athletic physique and dashing good looks of an adventurer—strong-jawed, sun-bronzed, his unruly brown hair barely grayed at the temples.

But rather than an open-collar shirt with its sleeves rolled up, and a sidearm in a snap holster at his hip, O'Connell wore a tailored tweed jacket and rubber boots, a creel resting on his hip—the very image of a gentleman fisher.

"One o'clock, ten o'clock," he muttered, and he forced his forward cast only to catch himself in the seat of his pants; then he felt a hook bite into his neck.

"Oww!"

His wife, Evelyn, was supposed to be the clumsy one in the family—he always found it endearing that her grace and ease could occasionally be interrupted by an awkward move, but what could compare to his clumsiness right now? Plowing through the willows, trying to untangle his errant fly, the tippet breaking, a branch poking him in the eye, and then somehow he was flat on his ass on the stream bank, moisture leaching through the cloth like blood from his wounded dignity.

Eyes narrowing, his mouth a vicious slash in a pitiless face, he clawed at the wicker creel and fumbled for the Colt .45 revolver within.

Then he was at the edge of the peaceful stream, taking aim at the wiggling tails and his lip curled back as he said, "Bite on *this*, you bastards. . . ."

And he began blasting at the water, splashing himself in the face but not minding, smiling in grim satisfaction.

Who did these damn fish think they were dealing with, anyhow?

When O'Connell, at the wheel of his 1939 Phaeton convertible, rolled through the gates of the palatial estate he shared with Evelyn, the majesty of his Tudor-style manor house and the luxuriant green expanse of its grounds made no impression on him. He had become used to living in a house that had more rooms than your average hotel. This was simply home to him, and he took it for granted.

Truth be told, a sort of ennui had recently settled in for O'Connell, now that the war was over and the jobs he and Evy had done for MI-5 were behind them. Nor had there been any talk of any new archaeological digs in Egypt or anywhere else, now that Evy was writing again, when she wasn't helping out at the British Museum. They were after her to be curator again, and he knew she was tempted.

But where did that leave him? What did an adventurer do, in retirement? *Was* this retirement . . . ?

O'Connell, arms filled with fishing tackle, let himself in; he was still soaking wet and the fly remained in his neck. "*Evy!* I'm home!"

Jameson, his veddy British, veddy bored butler, materialized to lend a hand and say, "Mrs. O'Connell is at her book reading, sir. She is expected home for dinner."

"Swell." O'Connell thrust the creel at the unflappable fellow. "We're having fish."

Climbing out of his tweed jacket, O'Connell caught the butler hefting the creel, doing a little weight estimate on its contents. "What, you didn't think I was going to catch anything?"

"Sir," the butler said, "I had the utmost confidence in your abilities. And from the feel of things, as you Americans are wont to say, you've made a real haul."

O'Connell grinned and was heading to the front closet, to hang up his coat and deposit his fishing gear, when the butler cleared his throat. O'Connell turned, and the butler discreetly gestured to a spot on the back of his master's neck.

Remembering the fly still stuck in the flesh back there, O'Connell said, "Oh, yeah. When you've taken as many slugs as I have, it's easy to forget about a little snag. Could you get me the wire cutters?"

"Certainly, sir."

The spacious front closet was the Elephant's Burial Ground of O'Connell's fallen hobbies—tennis and squash rackets, badminton set, rugby balls, cricket bats, bird-watching binoculars, shotgun cabinet replete with upland game-bird guns—and now the fishing gear joined these failed attempts at battling boredom.

Hung neatly on the side wall of the closet was his French Foreign Legion uniform. Wistfully, he stroked the striped pants, but before the flood of memories could begin, he stepped back and slammed the doors shut.

He'd been twenty or so when he'd won that battlefield commission. Not much older than his son, Alex, if any older at all. . . .

And now Alex was grown and gone, out of the house, across the ocean, making his mother proud at Harvard, or anyway the boy better be making her proud. Of course, right now Evelyn was out of the house, too, at another of these literary events. He wished he could share the excitement, but tea and crumpets and book talk were not exactly his style.

Funny thing, in the couple's heyday? Hadn't been Evy's style, either.

At Foyles bookstore on Charing Cross Road, an enthusiastic group of women—young, old and in between (but mostly young)—had gathered for a book signing (and reading!) by an author whose first two novels had made bestseller lists on both sides of the

Pond, although critics had been less than kind in either country.

Had the signing been set for the evening, and not the afternoon, an equal number of men might well have been in attendance, for Evelyn O'Connell's adventurous romances were the rare novels enjoyed equally by both sexes. The covers of those books may have indicated why: artwork suitable for American pulp magazines depicted a young blonde heroine being menaced by a shambling mummy while a young blond hero, square of jaw and blazing of gun, moved in to save her.

Each of the novels—*The Mummy* and *The Mummy Returns*—had its own pyramidal stacked display on either side of a lectern where the lovely author stood, reading. Her dustjacket photos, as glamorous as any movie star's, may have been another reason the male audience responded so well. . . .

But today in attendance were primarily women, who could identify with the slender, brown-eyed beauty before them, although unlike the heroine on her covers, the authoress was brunette. Her cream-color hat at a rakish angle, her gray-and-white suit as stylish as it was tasteful, she was as dignified as the covers of her novel were not.

And her audience hung on her every word.

" 'Now safely aboard the airship,' " Evelyn O'Connell said, " 'Scarlet and Dash marveled as the pyramid was swallowed into the swirling sandstorm. With the

32

mummy finally vanquished, Dash swept Scarlet into his arms. "Oh God, Scarlet. I thought I'd lost you." She returned his tender gaze and offered a whispered reply: "For a moment there, you had." Bathed in the rays of golden sunlight, the adventurer took the librarian into his strong, tired arms, and they shared a long, hard, passionate kiss worthy of a Knight Templar and an Egyptian Princess, their love deeper and truer than ever.' " She closed the cover. " 'The end.' "

She lifted her eyes to the crowd, smiling as they applauded, though one who knew her well might have detected a melancholy tinge to her expression. Reading aloud from her novels was always a bittersweet experience, because it took her back to a vital time in her life, and Rick's . . . but a time that was ever receding into the past. . . .

A young woman up front raised her hand and Evelyn nodded.

"Mrs. O'Connell," she said, standing, clearly nervous and starstruck. "We're all aware, of course, of your background as an Egyptologist, and that your husband, Richard, is a noted explorer."

Evelyn's smile widened. "He might prefer 'soldier of fortune.' "

That elicited rather more laughter than it deserved, Evelyn thought.

"What we're all dying to know," the woman said, "is whether the character of Scarlet O'Keefe is really you? *Based* on you?"

She paused and considered, as if she hadn't been asked this question scores of times. "Every writer of a novel is writing a hidden autobiography, it has been said. But I hate to disappoint you—honestly, I can say she's a completely different person." She cocked her head and turned on the practiced charm. "I mean, honestly—do you really believe my husband and I *actually* went around chasing, and being chased by, reanimated mummies?"

Laughter and applause followed this response, and she answered more of the standard questions ("Did you like Hollywood's version of your novel?") with her standard responses ("Very much . . . but you know, the book is *always* better"). Most of the women already had the first novel, and had brought it along for her signature, and every single one bought the new book, the sequel.

All in all, a very satisfying event.

Why, she wondered, *don't I feel happier about it?*

The grand O'Connell estate, by midevening, appeared from the road almost asleep, with only the kitchen and dining-room lights on.

Casual in a light blue blouse and dark trousers, Evelyn, waiting for dinner to be served, sat going through a small stack of mail from a silver tray. Rick entered, in a tie but no jacket, and she offered him her cheek to peck. He did so, if rather dutifully. He went over to a sideboard and poured himself a drink—

single malt (Oban thirty-year) and poured her a glass of sherry.

"Isn't this blissful?" she said. "A quiet dinner at home."

"Sure is."

"Remember when that was a rarity?"

"Yeah. Now it's every night."

He brought her the glass of sherry, they clinked drinks, and he said, "To retirement."

She beamed up at him. "May we stay this happy forever."

But as her husband stood there, swirling his drink and staring down into it, she wondered if he felt as bored and frustrated with their current life as she did.

"Still no letter from Alex," she said, back to going through mail. "You know, I've sent him three in the last month."

"What did you expect?" He grunted a laugh. "That kid only writes when he gets kicked out of college . . . or needs money."

"That's not fair, dear. I'm sure he's just got his nose buried in his books. Study, study, study."

"This is *Alex* we're talking about?"

She gave him a reproving smile.

He shrugged a little, and sat across from her at the big table and said, "How was your literary do?"

"Fine. We sold thirty-five copies of the new book and twenty of the old."

"Is that good?"

"It's excellent."

"And the question-and-answer session?"

She smirked at him. "Fine . . . until they asked me whether there'll be another mummy adventure." She shook her head. "You know, I really should be writing *serious* books, painstakingly researched nonfiction, or at the very least articles for academic journals. I'll lose my standing, and will never get back to the British Museum."

He tilted his head and gave her a look. "You did promise the publisher a third book. You signed a contract."

"I know," she sighed. "But I spend my nights staring at a blank page. This is that writer's block you hear so much about, apparently."

"What's the problem?"

"You *know* what the problem is—my novels were successful because I was drawing from personal experience. How can I make up a 'mummy' story out of whole cloth?"

He smirked. "It probably wouldn't be whole cloth. More like cloth full of holes . . . mummy wrappings? Get it?"

"I get it. And I appreciate you trying to lighten my mood. But I tell you, Rick, I am completely blocked."

He got that flirtatious grin going that she knew so well. "Well, if you need *inspiration* . . . how about we skip dinner and go straight to dessert? Maybe *I* can inspire you . . . upstairs?"

She laughed lightly. "That's very sweet of you, darling, but before any fun and games, I simply have to sit down in front of that typewriter until something exciting happens on the page."

She saw the twinge of disappointment in his eyes, but he was good enough not to press the matter.

The butler, Jameson, and a female servant in livery entered to place silver platters in front of Evelyn and Rick, who lifted lids simultaneously on two perfectly poached, championship-quality trout.

Her eyes and mouth were wide. "Why, Rick . . . this is *lovely*. I'm impressed, I really am." She beamed at him and he shrugged, aw shucks. "I'm delighted you've finally found a hobby that satisfies you . . . and one that for once does *not* involve guns."

She forked a mouthful of the delicate fish and the taste of it on her tongue was heavenly. She began to chew, and—*ouch!*—clamped down on something terribly hard.

Delicately, she removed an object from her mouth and regarded it quizzically. Was it a spent *bullet*? She dropped it on her Wedgwood plate with a clunk and looked across at Rick, who was grinning sheepishly.

"What can I say?" he said with a shrug. "He put up a hell of a fight."

Evelyn maintained a corner of the library as her office. Around her on the walls and here and there on the desk, to help encourage her muse, were mementos of their Egyptian adventures.

Shortly after dinner, she had typed the following deathless prose: *The sunset painted the Nile the color of blood,* and here she had stopped. She contemplated whether she'd used the word *the* too many times in one sentence. She wondered whether it might be better: *Sunset painted the Nile as red as blood.* Or perhaps: *Sunset painted the Nile blood red.*

These last two attempts, unlike the dozen or so crumpled sheets in her overflowing wastebasket, did not even make it onto paper. And this sheet soon joined the other wadded-up ones in (and around) the basket.

The problem was, whether the Nile was red or blue or purple wasn't the point. The point was, she had no story, and no experiences from which to create or even embellish one. The only decent idea she had involved the work she and Rick had done for the intelligence people during the war, exciting stuff, rivaling anything from the Imhotep days, or darn near.

Only that was classified, all of it.

That left her with only her imagination, and when it came to being imaginative, Evelyn Carnahan O'Connell was about as imaginative as your average scholar or museum curator, both of which she was.

She glanced up, hoping for inspiration, and her eyes landed on the Carnahan family shield on the wall—she had positioned this, with its two crossed swords, as another means of sparking her creativity. She stood and plucked a sword from its perch, savored its grip, then sliced the air with enthusiasm and skill.

Soon she was capering around the room like Tyrone Power in *The Mark of Zorro*, grinning as she parried an invisible foe across the wood-paneled library, her face flushed with excitement. Inspired, finally inspired, she leaped across a table, swung off a curtain, and decapitated a candle off the chandelier, yelling, "Take *that*!"

A cough behind her brought her down to earth, or at least to the parquet floor, and she tucked the sword behind her back, too late, because Jameson had obviously been standing in the doorway for a while now.

He said, "If there isn't anything else, madam, I should like to retire for the evening."

"Of course," a blushing Evelyn said. "Good night, Jameson. Sweet dreams."

"And you, madam."

She put things right, then returned to the desk and, rather than make another attempt, she straightened up her work area and took her leave of the library.

Upstairs, in her bathroom, she bathed and powdered herself and spritzed perfume in all the right places, and when she entered their bedroom in her sexiest robe, she was ready to be inspired.

But her husband wasn't in bed.

She slipped into the hallway and padded on bare feet to the staircase. From there she could see down into the study, where he sat in his favorite chair, its back to her as he faced the windows onto the garden. She tiptoed down and came up behind him and said, "Rick . . . is that offer still good? For a little inspiration?"

She dropped the robe and it pooled at her feet. She had bought the now-revealed sheer, silk negligee at Harrods and it had cost a small fortune; she'd been saving it for their anniversary, but some things just couldn't wait. . . .

She edged alongside the big comfy leather chair and touched his shoulder, rubbed his neck where it was always sore. "That time the mummy had me tied down, about to plunge his dagger into me . . . my heart was pounding. It's pounding like that now. Want to *feel* . . . ?"

His answer was a loud, abrupt, snort of a snore.

The great adventurer was asleep in his chair, his mouth open, a trickle of drool at one corner, the latest issue of a magazine devoted to guns and ammunition on his lap.

Guns could kill anything, she thought. *Even a mood.*

And she left him there.

The next afternoon, after a morning phone call requested a short-notice visit, the O'Connells received a valued colleague of the recent past in their sitting room. Jameson finished the tea service, and the couple, seated on a sofa, made small talk with their guest, who lounged across from them in a comfortable chair. Still, there was an air of near formality, Rick

O'Connell in a gray suit and dark tie, Evelyn in a lavender dress with a gold Egyptian symbol on a necklace.

Benjamin Fry—a lanky dark-haired man with sharp, almost hawkish features, and a palpable air of danger despite his three-piece-suit—sat with a small square mahogany box in his lap. *Were they to be presented a medal?* O'Connell wondered.

"The Foreign Office," Fry said, "appreciates all that the two of you did during the war . . . especially that nasty business in Luxor. But I've been sent to offer you, shall we say, one last assignment."

The couple, sitting close together, exchanged glances.

Then Evelyn shook her head, the brunette tresses bouncing on her shoulders, and said, "I'm afraid we've retired from the adventure business . . . *and* the espionage game." She smiled at her husband. "Haven't we, dear?"

O'Connell nodded assertively. "Absolutely! We are totally, completely, utterly retired." He swallowed. Sat forward just a little. "But out of respect to you, Benjamin, and since you made the trip out here . . . and, you know, just out of curiosity, maybe you could lay out the shape of the thing—not violating any state secrets, of course."

"Of course," Fry said. "Is that all right with you, Evelyn?"

"Certainly." She shrugged. "I can't see any harm in hearing why you asked for this meeting."

41

"It's a fairly straightforward job," he said. "Courier duty." He pointed to the mahogany box. "We would like you to deliver this to Shanghai. . . ."

O'Connell's eyebrows rose. "That?"

So did Evelyn's. "That box? What's in it?"

Fry, smiling just a little, perhaps already knowing he had them hooked, flipped the lid and light winked off the gem within in a thousand directions, a magnificent blue diamond gripped by a lattice of golden snakes rising from an oval plaque, nestled in velvet. The cut of the stone made myriad shades of blue: dark, light, the sea, the sky. . . .

"The blue hue, of course," Fry said, "results from trace amounts of boron in the stone's crystalline structure."

"Of course," O'Connell said. "However it got made, that's a nice slice of ice. Which Vanderbilt's engagement ring is that?"

The "slice of ice" had frozen Evy—not by the romance of such a stone or even its potential value; nor was this the reaction of the female of the species to a lovely jewel, rather that of a scholar, staggered, stunned, in awestruck recognition.

"It's the Eye of Shambhala," she said in hushed reverence. "Popularly known as the Eye of Shangri-la. My God . . ."

O'Connell, a hand on his wife's arm, frowned at her and said, "Stay-young-forever Shangri-la?"

She smiled at him, but her eyes were in some distant place. "Is there any other kind? If you believe the legend, that gem points the way to the Pool of Eternal Life."

"Which is, naturally," Fry said lightly, "Oriental poppycock. But I realize, Mrs. O'Connell, that such myths, such legends of magic, are of historical interest to you."

O'Connell nodded at the sparkling stone. "I have a historical interest, too. Like where did you get that hunk of junk?"

Evy frowned at him for this disrespect.

Fry took it in stride, however, and said, "The Eye was smuggled out of China in 1940—relatively recent history. Now, in these turbulent postwar times, we have a rare opportunity to show good faith to the Chinese government, who would very much like to see this artifact returned to their Shanghai Museum." To both of them, he said, "An old friend of yours is director there. Roger Wilson?"

O'Connell smirked. "No kidding? Leave it to ol' Roger to land on his feet again."

"Given your expertise in the field," Fry said, eyes first to O'Connell, then to Evy, "we naturally thought of you."

Evy shrugged. "But really, we'd just be a glorified delivery service. My training wouldn't enter in at all. Not that we aren't *flattered* . . . but Rick and I made a promise to each other that after the war we'd settle down."

Fry heaved a sigh. "Well . . . I must confess I'm disappointed. Postwar China is a dangerous, unpredictable place. With the Eye's unfathomable value on the black market, any number of factions could attempt to steal it, for political purposes, out of religious fanaticism . . . or frankly, just plain greed."

O'Connell shifted on the sofa.

So did Evelyn.

Fry said, "In lesser hands, the Eye could be lost forever."

"Well," Evelyn said, "we would hate for that to happen."

O'Connell began tapping a foot.

Fry said nothing.

Evelyn sneaked a look at her husband.

Finally O'Connell stuck in a toe: "Well, uh, you know Evy's brother, Jonathan, *does* live in Shanghai. Haven't seen him in some time. Could check up on him."

Fry smiled and nodded. "Yes, yes—he owns a night-club, if I'm not mistaken."

Evelyn gestured with open hands. "And we *have* been meaning to visit Jonathan. Maybe we could surprise him."

O'Connell was nodding. "It would make a perfect cover story."

Evelyn was nodding, too. "My thought exactly."

Fry twitched a smile. "Then I trust that means we can count on the O'Connells, one last time?"

After Fry had filled them in on the particulars, the couple showed him to the door and watched him drive off in a sleek black government limo.

"Do you hear that, Evy?"

"Hear what, Rick?"

Her hand was in his and he squeezed it. "That's adventure calling."

·❦ 2 ❦·

Colossal Beauty

Ningxia Province, China

The landscape could not have been less remarkable, a scrubby wasteland, a rolling near-desert
plain in the middle of nowhere, with one notable
exception—exposed from the sandy, barren expanse,
the slightly tilted head of a Sphinx-size giant appeared to peek above the surface as if the earth were
water and he a swimmer.

But had this been water, not earth, this "swimmer"
would have sunk like the stone he was, a brown, ancient representation, on a massive scale, of an ancient
ruler from 200 BC. This colossus had once been the
symbol of Emperor Er Shi Huangdi's absolute power,
a man about whom history had little kind to say.

The excavation site was still in its early stages, a

handful of tents and wooden pulleys and other fundamental mechanisms there to help two crews of a dozen or so Chinese diggers each in what promised to be one of the major archaeological finds of the twentieth century. The man responsible was named O'Connell, but his first name was not Richard.

Alex O'Connell, twenty, and a fugitive from his education, stood atop a mound of moved earth to survey what had been done so far, dwarfed by the partially excavated bust of the onetime Emperor of China. *Had the real man's eyes been so cold,* Alex wondered, *under the peak of that battle helmet?*

Alex, a handsome, husky youth with his mother's heart-shaped face and his father's steel-blue eyes (and unruly brown hair), did not look like a Harvard sophomore, although he did allow himself a Boston Red Sox baseball cap, to shade him from an unforgiving sun.

He looked like Rick O'Connell, a quarter century before, in dusty apparel suited to an explorer—brown leather jacket over green shirt and khaki trousers with boots and, of course, a satchel of tools on a shoulder strap, a Browning nine-millimeter automatic on his hip. Right now he had a ragged five-day growth of beard that gave him more authority than most collegians playing hooky.

From time to time, he would refer to pages in a large, battered, leather-bound journal. He was supervising one of the crews of Chinese diggers. The other crew had uncovered a pair of stone stairways that indicated a structure was down under the still mostly concealed colossus. They had cleared both stairways and, with the judicious use of dynamite, had carved quite a hole at the base of the Emperor's bust.

He yelled down, in perfect Mandarin, *"Chu Wah, you find the door to that tomb yet?"*

The digger—as youthful as Alex himself—looked up and called, also in Mandarin, *"No boss! Still looking!"*

From behind him echoed a distant voice: "Alex O'Connell . . . !"

He turned and gazed out at the endless nothingness until a pack train of mules revealed itself in the heat shimmer.

Good, Alex thought with a smile. *Wilson's back!*

He called down in Mandarin to the workers, in the valley they had made: *"The professor will give one hundred U.S. dollars to the man who discovers the entrance!"*

That got a cheer out of them. He only hoped the guy who found the damn door didn't get killed by a coworker seeking the credit, and the hundred bucks.

Fifteen minutes later, Roger Wilson dismounted from his mule, obviously at least as weary as the animal; in his early sixties, Wilson had spent decades at dozens of sites for nearly as many museums, and he was yet to have truly made his mark.

The balding, white-haired Britisher wore an olive-colored shirt with suspenders and chinos and he too was layered with the dust of these near-desert conditions. He received a warm hug from Alex, patting the boy on the back and turning the melancholy line that was his mouth into a smile.

Alex grinned and said, in an English accent not unlike his mother's, "What a relief you're here. You're a couple of days late, Professor—I was beginning to think you'd run into bandits."

"Appreciate the concern, dear boy," Wilson said, and mopped his brow with a filthy hanky. "But it was nothing so glamorous—we simply had some minor difficulties lining up proper supplies."

Alex handed his mentor a canteen and the man gulped from it, then the professor's eyes took in the impressive strides in the excavation that had been made in his absence. "Very good, Alex. Fine work indeed."

"Thank you, sir."

He put a hand on Alex's shoulder. "You know, when I saw you standing on that mound, surveying your kingdom, so to speak . . ." He chuckled. ". . . I thought for a moment there I was looking at your father. You are *definitely* Rick O'Connell's son."

With half a grin, Alex said, "Let us hope after *this* discovery, he'll be known as *Alex O'Connell's* father."

Wilson's smile spoke of obvious affection and pride, and this Alex relished.

The professor, hands on hips, appraised the partly exposed head of the colossus. "What a powerful gaze our friend has. . . . My colleagues at the museum were of course thrilled when I told them you'd discovered the Er Shi Huangdi Colossus—but they have the, uh, well, *usual* questions expected from those who fund such expeditions."

Alex smirked. "They want to know when I'm going to find the tomb. They want us to get in there and find the good stuff for them."

Wilson smiled, seemingly at Alex's frustration, the boy not realizing the professor found it amusing when Alex spoke idiomatically like his father in the cultured accent of his mother.

"Dear boy," he said, again placing a hand on Alex's shoulder, "you can't let the bureaucrats get you down. Not if you want to last in *this* game . . . You'll find the entrance, I know you will. I have the utmost confidence in you."

Alex grinned. "Thanks, Professor. You believing in me, well . . . it means a lot."

Their eyes met and the older man nodded and again a smile formed on the gruff, weathered face. Alex wondered why his own father didn't treat him with this kind of respect, or for that matter warmth.

The moment was interrupted by a shout from below. Alex and Wilson moved to where they could look down into the pit and saw Chu Wah looking up excitedly even as he pointed to what appeared to be the tomb's entrance, at the bottom of the sheer cliff of earth they'd excavated below the partially exposed Colossus.

"Boss!" Chu Wah yelled in Mandarin. *"I found*

51

the door, boss!" Then in English: "I get hundred smackers, right?"

Alex laughed and called down: "You do indeed!" Then to Wilson he said, "Grab the dynamite! They've found the entrance. . . . By the way, you owe Chu Wah a hundred bucks."

"I do?"

"You do."

Alex slipped the battered leather-covered journal into his satchel as he charged off, leaving Wilson to ponder how he'd managed to incur this debt, not having been here.

Within minutes, Alex was back, and he moved the older man to a safe position, and advised him to cover his ears, which he did. So did Alex, and then a huge explosion shook the plains and sent dirt and rock spewing upward, as if the earth had spit out a distasteful mouthful.

With another grin, Alex turned to his mentor and asked, "Ready to make history, Professor?"

Wilson chuckled. "Indeed I am. I have waited a very, very long *time* to make it. . . ."

And they headed toward stairs that had been installed over two thousand years before, by slaves whose bones had become one with the earth the modern-day diggers had just disrupted.

With a flashlight in his gloved hand, Alex led the way into the mausoleum with Wilson just behind him, followed by Chu Wah and a pair of Chinese diggers. Shafts of daylight slanted like swords in a magician's box through the deadfall of beams and structure caused by the blast. Despite the dynamite-created clutter, the space was too large and too dark to see much of anything. No one had set foot in here for many centuries . . .

. . . so why did Alex sense something was wrong?

"Move!" he said, but Wilson froze, and Alex had to grab the older man and yank him forward, just as two huge wooden arms, each affixed with a spiked plate, swung down from the ceiling, smacking together like huge cymbals right where the professor and his prize pupil had been standing.

The only victim, fortunately, was Alex's baseball cap, though one might also mark the nerves of Chu Wah and his diggers as casualties, the workers exchanging looks of alarm and muttering in Mandarin.

To the wide-eyed Wilson, Alex said, "Apparently the Emperor wasn't big on houseguests." Then in Mandarin he said, *"Stay together!"*

They stayed together, all right, cautiously descending a long, impossibly wide stone stairway with many massive stone beams at landings every dozen steps or so. The feel, now, was that of a temple, rife with Chinese carvings and figures on the walls. At the next landing, a shadowy figure could be glimpsed, mostly hidden in back of the beam just below, as if lying in wait for them, positioned to pick them off.

Alex stopped his little party with an upraised hand. He frowned. No one else had been in this mausoleum for several thousand years, right? Or had someone with his own agenda slipped inside right after the explosion—a religious fanatic maybe. . . .

Alex withdrew his sidearm and called, "You can come out now. We see you."

No answer.

With another upraised hand, he gestured for Wilson and the others to hang back on the stairs; then Alex went on down to the next landing. When he cocked the nine-millimeter Browning, the small sharp sound seemed deafening.

Stepping around the stone pillar carefully, nose of his gun paving the way, he could see the figure standing there, but slumped; and then his flashlight showed him who—or what—their one-man welcoming committee really was: a skeletal corpse. Its head bowed under a safari hat, the very old corpse was stuck to the beam, impaled by an Oriental throwing knife. On the rotting khaki shirt were initials: *CB*.

"It's all right!" Alex called, his voice echoing, and the others joined him on the landing. He turned to Wilson. "Sir Colin Bembridge, almost certainly."

Wilson frowned. "How in God's name did he get in here?"

"I don't know. Must be a way in we don't know about."

The head of the Bembridge Scholars was known to

have gone searching for the tomb of Er Shi Huangdi, making several expeditions, the last one some seventy years ago, from which he never returned.

"Well," Wilson said, nodding toward Alex's satchel, "you can thank the old boy for that journal of his."

If Alex hadn't discovered the long-forgotten book in the archives of the library at Harvard, this expedition would not have happened.

"Thanks," Alex said softly to the corpse.

He lifted the safari hat by its brim and the skull rolled off and down the stairs, making little clunks as it went; the absence of the skull revealed (stuck in the stone) an oversized bronze throwing star.

"Somebody left him here," Alex said, his gut wrenching with sympathy for the poor bastard, "as a warning."

"Unfortunately for Sir Colin," Wilson said, "he's not the dead man we're looking for. *He* won't make us rich and famous. . . . Let's keep moving, shall we?"

Alex nodded, but his first step depressed a floor tile, setting something strange and wonderful in motion: dumping accumulated sand, skylights slid back one by one, allowing shafts of sunlight to cascade down, thanks to the dynamite clearing away much of the roof of the mausoleum.

Now the awestruck group got a sense of the enormity of their find. The space was vast and entirely covered by an array of terra-cotta warriors, many with terra-cotta horses, standing at attention and lined up on wooden-plank flooring to stretch into the dimmest recesses of the mausoleum. Oddly, the soldiers seemed arranged to face a large open space at their center. . . .

Beside Alex, Wilson said, "Incredible . . . no two faces are alike. Can you imagine how long it must have taken to cast all these? What sort of artists they must have had!"

Alex shook his head. "Not artists, if the ancient legends are to be believed—more like sorcerers."

"Surely you can't believe that."

But he did. He had reason to. He said, "They weren't cast, Professor—trust me, they were cursed."

Wilson snorted a laugh. "Don't tell me you actually believe such mystical poppycock! What sort of tales did your parents tell you at bedtime? Oh, don't remind me—I've heard the wild stories flying around Cairo about your parents, and mummies being raised from the dead to walk among us."

They did more than just walk, Alex thought. He had been there—he had been Imhotep's prisoner, and he had fought side by side as a boy of ten, with his father, to defeat the Mummy and his minions. But in his mind he could see his mother, with a finger to her lips in *shush* fashion: "Family secret, Alex. Family *secret . . .*"

"Professor," Alex said, "you have really got to stop reading my mummy's mummy books."

Wilson, interested neither in puns nor curses, moved

56

ahead, and Alex fell in with him, the Chinese trio behind them. In awe, the party walked down an aisle between uniform rows of terra-cotta soldiers and horses. Their flashlights cut the dust-mote-filled air like blades.

They trod on, in cathedral-like silence, until Chu Wah stepped on another tile, triggering a blast of yellow gas that shot up from the floor and into his startled face. He began to choke and gag and do a terrible dance, his skin blistering horrifically.

And then he collapsed.

"Chu Wah!"

Quickly Alex went to his loyal crew captain and knelt and checked for a pulse.

Too late.

"Poor bugger's dead," Alex said, looking up at the professor, who frowned but said nothing.

None of the party could see, nearby in the shadows, an ancient seismograph with bronze balls resting delicately on its lids. The commotion Chu Wah made dying had shaken the lid and the balls thereon, which were now rolling to fall off and into a bronze frog's mouth. . . .

A ratchet sound echoed in the chamber.

Alex rose from the corpse of his crew captain and looked around as the grinding sound continued.

And when it stopped, crossbow bolts *thwacked* as dozens of arrows flew from the darkness like strafing machine-gun fire. Alex was right in their path, and Wilson yelled for him to run, and he did, but the Chinese digger just behind Alex was nailed by a volley and pinned to the floor, the sharp arrows ripping through him, killing him before he could even cry out.

High in the dark recesses of the chamber, racks of crossbows on gimbals sent arrows raking blindly to kill any living thing that dared violate the sacred aisles below. Alex ran, the arrows seemingly chasing him, flurries of them landing just behind him as he pressed forward into the gloom. Wilson was running, too, and the surviving digger.

Then the arrows seemed to have stopped.

But another ratcheting noise announced another volley, this time of the razor-sharp throwing disks, like the one that had dispatched Bembridge so many years ago.

Alex called, *"Duck!"*

Wilson dove behind a terra-cotta warrior, who was decapitated in short order. The remaining digger caught a star deep in his chest, and flipped backward, dead before he hit the floor. At the same time, Alex dove as one of the buzz-saw-like disks flew almost close enough to give him the shave he needed.

Again the mausoleum fell quiet.

No one moved for what seemed a very long time, but was actually a matter of seconds. Finally Wilson peeked out cautiously. He and Alex were the only ones left alive, and Alex—tucked behind a terra-cotta horse—felt not at all cocky at the moment, his self-confidence drained out of him like blood from a wound.

Nonetheless, the young man rose and strode out and over to the final of the diggers, on his back with that disk sunk into his chest, a spreading red blossom on his tunic around the deadly steel star. Alex knelt next to the man, and checked his pulse just to be sure.

Wilson came up. "He's dead, son. There's not a thing in the world you can do for him."

Alex stared at the dead man. He remembered seeing him laughing and drinking with his fellow diggers the night before, vital, alive. "He's dead because of me, Professor. All *three* are dead because of me."

Alex got to his feet and punched one of the terra-cotta warriors in the face, crumbling its head.

Wilson took the distraught young man by the shoulders and faced him, sternly but not unkindly. "Danger of this sort comes with the territory, lad. You know that better than most."

Alex swallowed and nodded. He pushed the guilt down so he could get back to the work at hand.

Wilson clapped his hands. "Now! Let's find the crypt, and make sure these poor sods didn't die in vain."

They walked into the open central space, the bare area that the terra-cotta warriors were lined in rows to face.

Alex squinted. "All the warriors are arranged as if they're waiting for an order from their emperor."

Wilson nodded. "Agreed. But then . . . where the hell *is* he? There's no statue, no coffin. Or did some grave robbers beat us to the prize?"

"I don't think so." Alex stepped to the middle of the circle and, with his foot, wiped sand away. "He's still here."

Excitement rushing through him, Alex reached into the satchel on its shoulder strap and whipped out an archaeological brush. He got on his hands and knees and began to dust off the floor, quickly revealing bowls carved into the floor surrounded by Chinese figures, all inset in a circular stone.

"They locked him in," Alex said, "using the five Chinese elements . . ." He gestured to the bowls, one by one. "Water, earth, metal, wood, fire." He looked up at the professor. "It's configured like a compass, but not just any compass—a feng shui one. . . . Professor, please, shine your torch this way."

Wilson, standing nearby, held his flashlight so that Alex could get out his own compass from a pants pocket. "This is true north, but the compass is set in the opposite direction—we need to realign it."

Using the bowls as handholds, the two men strained to revolve the stone, trying to make a wheel of it. When the stone clicked into place, an ancient mechanism rumbled . . . and the entire circular floor split apart, like a giant hinged trapdoor.

Scrambling, Wilson managed to roll off and save himself, but Alex fell into the newly revealed crevasse, taking a nasty hit on the rump of a bronze horse and bouncing off to find his face in someone else's face.

Someone else who had been dead for a very long time.

Pushing the mummified corpse away, and getting to his feet, a horrified Alex used his flashlight to identify three mummies, arms around one another. Based upon their feminine garb, Alex deduced that these were concubines the Emperor had buried with him.

Wilson called down, "Are you all right, son?"

Alex said, "Fine!"

Then Alex swung his flashlight around and was confronted by the find of a lifetime.

"Oh . . . my . . . *God* . . ."

"Dear boy, what *is* it?"

"Nothing much. Just the greatest discovery since my grandfather found King Tut. . . ."

A ceremonial bronze chariot, drawn by four magnificent bronze horses, stood connected to an even larger cortege wagon on which rested an ornate sarcophagus; the entire affair perched on a platform. Commanding the chariot was a slightly oversized bronze figure of the Emperor—even in bronze, Er Shi Huangdi's face radiated a fierce cruelty and a dark charisma.

The scale of it all dwarfed the young explorer.

61

Millennia of blackness had shrouded these impressive objects, and now his eyes were on them.

Above, kneeling over the edge of the crevasse, Wilson clenched a fist and said, "Finally! At last . . . at last . . . *yes!*"

But before his victory could be relished, Wilson was sent into a black pit—not that of the crevasse before him, rather into unconsciousness, thanks to a vicious kick in the head from an assailant so silent, the professor hadn't heard even a whisper of approach.

In the Emperor's crypt below, Alex was unaware of the attack on his mentor. Right now he was climbing up a chariot wheel to get at the sarcophagus, the top of which he dusted off with a gloved hand, revealing a bas-relief of a three-headed dragon.

The Emperor's symbol!

Now Alex knew for sure—this was indeed Er Shi Huangdi's final resting place.

Pleased with himself, the young explorer jumped down. His flashlight traveled to the various mummified figures, including the concubines. *Horny selfish bastard,* he thought. *Even had his lovelies buried alive with him.*

His attention elsewhere, Alex did not see the lithe, masked figure in black drop silently down into the crypt, behind him.

He turned just as the assassin was blending into the darkness, and called up, "Professor Wilson! You want to come down and have a look?"

Nothing.

Grinning, Alex called, "What's wrong, Professor? So overwhelmed by the prospect of fame and fortune, you can't even find the words? It's not like you!"

Craning to try to catch a glimpse of his mentor, Alex presented a perfect target for the intruder, who hooked a kick around and caught him in the neck, knocking the boy hard against a bronze horse's rump. Alex shook the blow off and drew his nine-millimeter automatic, but a foot whipped out and flicked it away. He heard the gun clunk somewhere across the crypt, but between him and the weapon was a barrier . . .

. . . an assassin in black, from turban to toe.

And that assassin was unsheathing a dagger with a dragon hilt.

With lightning speed, the assassin attacked, dagger in hand, but Alex ducked with similar speed, and the blade sparked off the bronze animal, momentum bringing the assassin forward enough to give Alex the opportunity to kick the figure behind the knee. Then the young explorer dove onto the floor, like he was stealing a base, to slide through an array of bones and skulls to retrieve his gun.

Alex plucked up the Browning and thumbed back the hammer and began firing, only the assassin was the moving target to end all moving targets, backflipping behind the chariot, the bullets digging noisy holes in support beams as Alex emptied his clip. One stray bullet cut through the rope of a huge granite counterweight and an ominous grinding groaned through the crypt.

The floor—actually the platform of the monument—began to rise, chariot and all.

Alex had an empty handgun now, and his extra clips were in his satchel, which had come off his shoulder during the fracas and was likely still below, as the platform slowly raised. He edged around the chariot, hoping to surprise the assassin, who surprised Alex instead, swinging between two bronze horses to kick the boy back, almost off the platform, which was perhaps five feet off the ground now.

Now the figure in black faced the husky young explorer and each began to circle and assess their respective foes; the appraisal period was a short one, as feet and fists began to fly, in a martial-arts test of wills, limited only by the relatively small area of the rising platform dominated by the chariot, bronze horses, and cortege wagon.

Alex had an apparent advantage—he towered over his foe, and definitely had the reach and the weight; but his opponent was wily and lithe, and seemed to anticipate his every blow. Of course the same could have been said about Alex, because blows and blocks were evenly traded in blurs of speed that challenged the eye.

Backflipping over the low point, where the chariot was tethered to the cortege wagon, the assassin seemed to have retreated; but then almost magically reappeared, leaping over the chariot to grab Alex in a flying scissors that took both of them down, hard, raising a cloud of dust. As this ancient elevator continued to rise, Alex found himself with his head hanging over the platform's edge, the counterweight on its way down to smash his head like a damn two-minute egg!

The assassin swung the dagger down to stab him, but Alex knocked the knife-in-hand out of the way; as they struggled, Alex could see only that counterweight, maybe two feet above his face, inexorably lowering itself. He got a hold of his opponent's turban and yanked, snapping the guy's head back. Finally Alex could roll away from the platform's edge—they were a good eight feet up now—the counterweight brushing his hair . . . *too close!*

Then he leaped to his feet, the flung dragon dagger also just missing him, whizzing past him to *thunk* deep into the wooden side of the cortege wagon.

That's a bloody 'nuff, he thought, and threw an American-football-style block into the assassin, knocking the guy into a wagon wheel on the cortege. He wrapped his hands around the assassin's throat and lifted him off the floor by the neck, then removed a hand to whip off the black mask . . . and it was no *"guy,"* no *"him,"* at all!

He was now staring into the defiant eyes of a Chinese beauty, a slender young woman not much older than Alex, if at all. Her face was oval with symmetrical features, her almond eyes large and dark, her nose aquiline, her lips full and sensuous. Had she not just tried to kill him a dozen times, it might have been love at first sight.

Maybe it was, anyway.

"You're a girl?" he asked, not exactly a question worthy of a Harvard man.

Her only reply was to use the momentary stasis to find her leverage and position her feet in the wagon spokes behind her. She thrust forward and butted him in the head and set herself free as she sent him reeling.

She vaulted over him, along the way grabbing the hilt of the embedded dragon dagger to free it from the wooden cortege wagon, and landed nimbly. She'd barely touched down when shots rang out and echoed through the mausoleum.

Wilson was above as the platform rose to him, and he was firing at the girl, who leaped off the platform and up and out, disappearing through the rows of terracotta warriors and into the darkness of the vast tomb.

Alex said, "That's enough," but the professor was already clicking on an empty chamber.

The platform had risen to floor level now, bringing the chariot monument and the sarcophagus to their rightful position among the thousands of clay warriors.

Alex, feeling groggy from hand-to-hand combat the likes of which he'd never known before, looked to Wilson quizzically. "Where *is* she?"

"You might well ask . . . *what* is she?"

And the young man and the older one stood staring into the darkness, and neither sight nor sound of the lovely assassin was forthcoming.

·❦ 3 ❦·

Everybody Comes to Jonathan's

Shanghai, China

Not much more than a year before, Shanghai—China's leading city and one of the world's busiest seaports—had been under Japanese rule. By now it had resumed its rightful position as a citadel of wickedness, where monied Europeans rode in American cars past the poverty of market-choked streets and alleys zigzagged with lanterns and washing lines. Shanghai police on their way to quell rioting factory workers would rumble down neon-washed avenues along which platoons of prostitutes offered their wares outside posh hotels while fireworks celebrated the opening of yet another nightclub.

One such nightclub bore a neon sign that flashed the word IMOHTEP'S. Two Chinese doorman in full livery waited to welcome wealthy visitors to an elegant interior invoking an art moderne Egyptian fantasy. Even the Asian barmaids invoked sensual exotic dreams, their lovely flesh covered with wisps of cloth but mostly body paint.

A bartender had compared the nubile young women wearing black blunt-cut bangs to Cleopatra herself, but Jonathan Carnahan—the proprietor of Shanghai's latest favorite nightclub among the elite tourist trade—had in fact patterned the barmaids' distinctive look after that of another ancient Egyptian princess: Anck-su-namun.

Legend had it, Anck-su-namun had been the Pharaoh Seti's concubine of choice, at least until she murdered him, and then took her own life, knowing her lover, the great High Priest Imhotep, would raise her from the dead. Of course, Jonathan knew this to be more than a legend, having met both Anck-su-namun and Imhotep personally, and *not* thirteen hundred years ago. . . .

Considering what travails Jonathan, his sister, Evy, and his brother-in-law, Rick O'Connell, had been through, thanks to Imhotep and that nasty piece of Egyptian business called Anck-su-namun, the last thing Jonathan should want to do was surround himself with images that recalled those nearly fatal adventures.

But Jonathan was if nothing else an entrepreneur, and the publicity he and the O'Connells received, both from their Egyptian finds and then the popular novels his sister had written (which featured a dashing second lead not unlike a certain Jonathan Carnahan), had made Imhotep's (and its Valley Nile decor) a natural.

He raised his cocktail glass as if toasting his wealthy patrons. "To Imhotep," he said to no one in particular. "May the bugger actually *stay* dead, this time. . . ."

Jonathan was in his late forties, but thanks to boyish features, looked younger, despite a certain tendency toward activities that might tend one to dissipation. His light brown hair was touched with surprisingly little gray, and his brown eyes were sharp and intelligent, though sometimes casually half lidded. Just under six feet, Jonathan, in his blue brocade tuxedo and black tie, made the perfect picture of a sophisticated nightclub owner.

He was sipping his drink when he spotted his tuxedo-sporting nephew, Alex O'Connell—*My, the lad cleans up well,* he thought—coming down the stairs from the entryway into the club, carrying himself with a confidence worthy of either of his celebrated parents.

With amusement and perhaps a little pride, Jonathan watched as a beautiful brunette heiress from New York floated over to his nephew, her charms spilling from a low-cut gown.

Jonathan was close enough to hear the conversation that followed.

"Hello, handsome," she said.

Not exactly a brilliant opening gambit, Jonathan thought. But a woman who looked like that did not need to sound like a character out of Noël Coward. She was dangerous, though, a slightly soiled debutante who gave a whole new meaning to "The Lady Is a Tramp."

She was saying, "Just get into town?"

"Yeah," Alex said, with a brash smile. "I've been out west on an archaeological expedition."

She cocked her head and narrowed her eyes as she squeezed his nearer arm. "That sounds fascinating. Maybe we could find somewhere quiet, and cover some unexplored territory of our own."

The boy's confidence fizzled. "Well, uh, er, ah . . ."

Jonathan frowned. *Didn't they teach these college boys* anything *over in the States?*

She was working a gloved hand along Alex's chest when Jonathan decided he needed to swoop in and save the lad from a fate worse than death. Well, perhaps not worse than death . . . actually quite a nice fate, unless one of her other boyfriends was around . . . still . . .

Jonathan moved in, slipped an arm around his nephew's shoulder, and gave the heiress a pick-on-someone-your-own-size smile, to which she responded with a mind-your-own-business frown, and walked the lad toward the bar.

"Alex, my boy," Jonathan said. "Let your uncle buy you a drink. . . ."

Alex was craning to look at the brunette ship he seemed to be passing in the night. "Well, that's swell of you, Uncle Jon, only that young lady seems to have the same idea . . . and to be honest, she's better-looking than you."

They were at the bar now.

"That's a matter of perspective," Jonathan said, "and trust me, old son, there isn't much virgin territory to be explored on that continent. Let me put it in archaeological terms—that's one tomb in which many a pharoah has lain. . . . Tell me, have you given any thought to how you'll handle your parents, when they find out what you've been up to of late?"

Alex shook his head and smirked sourly. "It's not my fault that they got out of the family business."

Jonathan ordered up a cocktail for himself and a Coca-Cola for his nephew; this may have been Shanghai, but the lad was still only twenty. "My boy, your discovery will be all over the press in a matter of days—papers, radio, newsreels. Your father may not be a genius, but even he will be able to add two to two and come up with four . . . 'four' being the simple fact that you have dropped out of college."

The brunette wandered by, flashing Alex a smile. Virgin territory or not, the boy seemed interested in planting a flag for Great Britain.

"Alex! Pay attention. This is serious business. Can you imagine what your parents' reaction will be?"

Alex threw down half the Coke, frowned at it when he realized what it was, then said, "Relax, Uncle Jon. The chance of Rick and Evy O'Connell coming down those stairs is a million-to-one shot. Even *you* couldn't lose with those odds. . . ."

"Perhaps not."

"If you'll excuse me?" Alex made a face as he put the Coke glass on the counter. Then he moved toward the brunette, who had been lingering on the sidelines. A moment after he got to her, she grabbed him by the arm and dragged him into the adjoining room.

Jonathan sighed, then muttered to himself, "Boy's going to be eaten alive . . . although Lord knows there are worse ways to go."

The proprietor of Imhotep's sipped his martini and surveyed his kingdom languidly. The band was playing "Slow Boat to China," couples out on the dance floor clinging to each other. His eyes moved to the stairs and he saw a handsome couple coming down, a tall, broad-shouldered fellow in tuxedo and black tie, and a gorgeous, dark-eyed, dark-haired wench in a gold lamé gown. Jonathan was straightening his tie, taking in the woman's beauty, when the couple moved into the light and Jonathan thought, *Crikey, it's my sister!*

And the tall-broad shouldered fellow, of course, was his brother-in-law. *Of all the gin joints in all the towns of the world,* Jonathan thought, *they walk into mine. . . .*

He quickly turned his back to the newcomers.

But behind him, his sister called out, *"Jonathan!* Yoo-hoo!"

She'd spotted him. Yoo-hoo indeed.

He turned slowly and did his best to hide his unease, and failing pitifully, thinking, *I must have been a right bastard in my previous life,* saying, "I swear on our parents' graves I had no idea he was here!"

O'Connell frowned. *"Who* was here?"

A figure exploded out of the adjacent room— hurled from there in a blur of tuxedo and brown hair and indignation . . . specifically, the figure of Alex O'Connell.

Jonathan hadn't seen this, however, having turned his back, as if contemplating ordering another drink.

Nor could he see Rick O'Connell dividing a look-to-kill between Alex, on the floor in a heap getting gaped at by customers, and Jonathan, who also didn't see his sister, staring at him accusingly.

She demanded of the back of him, "How long has Alex been in China?"

Unaware he'd been busted, Jonathan said, "Alex, in China? I thought he was in America, studying. Are you *sure* he's in China?"

O'Connell said, "Pretty sure."

The couple moved away from Jonathan, just as he turned to see Evy helping Alex up from the nightclub floor. Jonathan closed his eyes, hoping it would all go away.

O'Connell followed his wife over to their wandering boy, whom she was fussing over, brushing him off as Alex stood there frozen in shock at the sight of his parents, who had seemingly materialized before him.

"Mom," Alex said. "Dad. What are *you* doing here?"

"Funny thing, kiddo," O'Connell said. "We were just going to ask you the same thing."

From the other room bounded a big guy in a brown jacket and khaki trousers, fists balled, eyes narrowed, mouth a violent slash in the midst of several days' growth of beard. The guy was clearly on the warpath, and zeroing in on Alex.

In a voice more than slightly touched with Irish, the strapping brute called behind him to friends still in the side room. "Be right back, lads! I just need to finish the job I started. . . ."

He bore in on Alex, who bunched his shoulders and raised his fists, ready to give back as good as he got; but when the Irishman cocked his arm to pummel the boy, O'Connell caught the man's fist.

The Irishman spun around, ready to take on a second "job," but when the two men were face-to-face, their features flashed with mutual recognition.

"Maddog?" O'Connell asked tentatively. "Maddog *Maguire*?"

Maguire frowned. "Ricochet? Ricochet Rick O'*Connell*?"

"You got old."

"You didn't get younger."

They seemed about to go at it, but instead fell into each other's arms, hugging, clapping each other on the back, clearly long-lost friends.

They separated, looking each other over, grinning.

O'Connell said, "Will you look at you? You're even uglier. How the hell's that possible? How long has it been, anyway?"

"Not so long, lad. Egypt. 'Twenty-three."

"We were in the French Foreign Legion together," O'Connell said, turning with a smile to his wife and son. "This damn maniac could land a plane on a postage stamp."

"They had planes back in those days, Dad?" Alex asked, openly sarcastic. "What, like in *King Kong*?"

Maguire tossed a thumb at Alex. "This scrapper's *your* kid, Rick?"

O'Connell nodded, then glanced over at the entry to the adjacent room, from which had emerged a group of men who were likely rough-and-tumble pilot pals of Maguire's, clearly wondering why Alex hadn't been pureed by now.

"As much as I'd like to let you and your boys teach Alex here a valuable lesson," O'Connell said, "it might tend to—"

"Upset his mother," Evy said. "Very much."

And she began brushing the boy off again, to his displeasure.

"Mom, *seriously*," Alex said, pulling away. "You're embarrassing me in front of my new friends."

That made O'Connell smile, and Maguire, too.

The pilot said, "Just tell your young laddie-buck here to keep his sweaty paws off my lass."

Alex gestured to himself. "To be strictly fair about it, your 'lass' had her hands all over *this* laddie-buck."

Evy frowned. "Alex!"

Maguire's upper lip drew back and a growl rumbled in his throat, but O'Connell slipped an arm around his old pal.

"Why don't you," O'Connell said chummily, "and your boys of course, head over to the bar."

"Why should we?"

"Because you're the lucky one-thousandth customer here at Imhotep's. You've just won you and your compadres a night of drinks on the house."

Jonathan, who had been keeping his distance over at the bar, perked up and came quickly over. "On the what? Who's counting bloody *customers*?"

Evy gave her brother a sharp elbow and a sharper look.

Jonathan's face blossomed in a smile. "Yes, of course! Anything for my loving little family."

Maguire broke out in a grin and held his hand out to O'Connell, who shook it. "Welcome to the Orient, Ricochet me lad."

"It's been fun so far."

Maguire and his boys, in rowdy good cheer, assembled at the bar and Jonathan closed his eyes in painful contemplation of dollars not going into his cash register.

O'Connell, no longer smiling, turned to face his son. "I'm not here five minutes and *already* I'm pulling your fanny out of the fire!"

"How hard was that?" Alex said with a shrug. "All you had to do was play the French Foreign Legion card."

O'Connell returned the shrug. "Well, like they say, 'Once a legionnaire, always a legionnaire.'"

"When was it they said that? The twenties? Right after they said twenty-three skidoo?"

O'Connell frowned at his son, wondering for a moment why he'd bothered rescuing him from Maguire and the other mad dogs. Maybe it was the boy's teeth, which had been straightened at some expense, and having them flung all over the nightclub floor would have been a pity, and a wasted investment.

But before any more sparks, or worse, could fly, Evy came over and stepped between father and son.

"Enough, you two!" To Rick she said, "You back down." To her brother she said, "You get us some drinks." To her son she said, "You have a lot of explaining to do, young man."

Jonathan remained at the bar while the O'Connell family reunion moved to a booth where they ignored a lavish Egypt Meets Hollywood floor show, and caught up on more important things.

O'Connell, after getting filled in by his son, frowned and said, "I thought we had a firm no-more-digging-up-mummies rule in this family."

Alex's eyebrows rose. "That's your rule, Dad. Anyway . . . I'm not planning to raise this one from the dead."

Keenly interested, Evy asked Alex, "Where *is* the late Emperor, at the moment?"

"The Shanghai Museum. We're waiting for official verification of the discovery. Really just a formality, Roger says."

"Roger," O'Connell said. "So Roger Wilson hired you?"

Alex nodded. "Roger was a visiting lecturer at Harvard. He looked me up, because he was friends with you and Mom. Said he'd talked to my instructors and was pleased by what he'd heard."

O'Connell's eyes flared. "So impressed he encouraged you to drop out of school?"

"Roger says he'll get me credit. It's what they call 'work study,' these days."

"Good ol' Roger arranged this with your instructors, then? You're on a kind of leave of absence?"

"Well . . . not exactly."

O'Connell sighed. Closed his eyes tight. "You *did* drop out."

Alex leaned forward. "Listen, the professor believed in me all the way—staked his reputation on it."

O'Connell said drily, "Well, we'll be sure to thank him."

But Evy was beaming with pride. "You do realize," she said to her son, "that with a discovery of this magnitude, the Bembridge Scholars will be knocking down your door."

The boy shook his head. "No, Mom. That's not my dream, working at a museum. *Yours* maybe . . . not mine."

That deflated and hurt her, though her son didn't notice. O'Connell did, however, and said, "So, then . . . what's *your* dream? What's *your* big plan?"

Alex shrugged. "I'd be lying if I said I had one. Look, I like to play it by ear, a little on the fast and loose side. I'm thinking maybe I'll just travel the world and seek my fortune . . . like you did."

"Those were different times," his father said. "And I was in a position where there was no choice but to make my own way. Son, the world is considerably more dangerous today than when I was your age."

Another shrug. "I'll take my chances."

Evy sat forward; her tone was sweet, not at all critical. "Dear, we were rather hoping you might go back to Harvard, and finish up. Maybe Roger can pave the way, as he said . . . ?"

Alex smiled, but more to himself than to his parents.

He shook his head. "Who told you I dropped out? Did the college contact you? How did you think this was going to work? You two would just show up and talk me out of it? Crash *my* adventure . . ."

O'Connell said, "We didn't know you were here."

"Dad . . . come on. . . ."

"Son, we weren't expecting to find you at all, considering we thought you were in school in Massachusetts."

With a suspicious glance at Jonathan over at the bar, Alex said, "Well, Uncle Jon knew, in case there was a problem or emergency or something."

Evy seemed hurt again. "You felt you could confide in your uncle, and not your parents? We have to trust each other, Alex—we can't keep hurtful secrets. This is not how a proper family behaves."

Alex's eyes widened; he grinned mirthlessly. "Proper family? We may be related, but we haven't been any kind of family, in a long, long time, much less a 'proper' one."

He shook his head and quickly climbed out of the booth.

From his vantage point at the bar, Jonathan saw this and followed Alex up the stairs and out past the doormen and onto the street, a world crammed with steaming food carts, rickshaws, pimps, beggars, and club hounds. The boy moved through the exotic bustle and his uncle clambered after him.

"*Alex!* Wait. . . ."

Alex turned slowly and faced his uncle.

"You need to give your folks a chance, my boy. You've thrown them quite a curve. . . ."

The boy shook his head, waved his arms. "They *never* change, Uncle Jon! You know what sort of discovery I've just made, and how do they react? They still treat me the same—like I'm ten years old!"

"Be fair—you caught them by surprise. And you weren't exactly supposed to be here now, were you?"

Alex sighed. "What the hell are they *doing* in Shanghai? Don't you think it's a little strange that they show up, just as I'm about to make my mark?"

Jonathan put a hand on the boy's shoulder. "I understand. Your parents *do* throw a long shadow. . . ."

"Are you kidding? More like a total eclipse . . ."

Jonathan squeezed his nephew's shoulder. "Come back inside, my boy. I've got some champagne on ice—to hell with Coca-Cola. Have a couple of glasses of the bubbly, and trust your old uncle—you *will* feel better."

But Alex only shook his head. "Sorry, Uncle Jon. Not tonight. Rain check."

And he turned and stalked off and was soon swallowed in the late-night throng.

Moments later, Evelyn and Rick O'Connell burst from the club onto the neon-drenched street.

O'Connell was right behind his wife, who was livid.

"This is all your fault!"

"*My* fault?" O'Connell shook his head in disbelief. "You're the one who constantly smothered that boy—couldn't leave him alone for five minutes without wiping his nose."

She wheeled and got in her husband's face. "Maybe I was overcompensating for the fact you never took any real interest in your son's life."

O'Connell's eyes popped. "Are you kidding? His life has *always* been my top priority. Do you have any idea how many times I stopped him from breaking his damn-fool neck?"

She put her fists on her hips. "Perhaps with a little warmth and encouragement, he might not have felt the need to show off for you. A little fatherly support would have gone a long way."

"Well . . . it was implied."

They said nothing for several long moments, just standing facing each other, mutually flummoxed, with the Chinese doormen as mute observers.

Finally Evy, shaking her head, said, "We've spent the better part of our lives finding priceless artifacts, you and I . . . and now the one thing that's most precious to us, we've lost."

O'Connell could say nothing to that.

Evy sighed. "We should never have sent him away to Australia."

Shrugging, O'Connell said, "He was fourteen! How were we supposed to keep him safe, with bombs blitzing London, and Nazis swarming Cairo? What other choice did we have?"

She considered that, then asked, "Is that really true?"

"Well, of course it is."

"Or is that just what we tell ourselves, to make it all right that we went off adventuring again?" She shook her head again, determination mingling with frustration edged with sadness. "I will not allow Alex to become some stranger in framed pictures on our mantel."

O'Connell drew in a deep breath, and then let it out. "Okay. So how do we fix this?"

"Frankly . . . I am not really sure. But I do know one thing."

"What, Evy?"

Her eyes met his and they were alone on the bustling street of neon-streaked Shanghai.

She said, "We need to do it together."

He swallowed and nodded and slipped an arm around her, and led her back inside the nightclub.

Neither of them was aware that from the shadows of the alley across the street, a tall, formidable-looking Chinese woman in her thirties in a slit-up-the-side silk dress—her lovely face marred by a scar—had been watching them with much more than casual interest.

·◖ 4 ◗·

Eye Opening

China–General Yang's Training Camp

Under a high, hot sun, an orderly arrangement of yurt-style tents encircled the sprawling ruins of an ancient Ming temple; carts of ammunition and weapons and other military gear were neatly stacked at various key points.

Nearby, platoons of Chinese mercenaries in gray uniforms representing no modern nation—bearing the insignia of Emperor Er Shi Huangdi's three-headed dragon—were engaged in a variety of training exercises, including target practice and close-order drill, displaying a precision that indicated these endeavors had been going on for quite some time now.

Through the training field rumbled a chauffeured jeep with a general in back, who received salutes from officers as the vehicle passed. This was General Yang, who also represented no nation, other than that of his own ambitions, his rank self-bestowed. A tall, slender yet round-faced man with thinning dark hair and a trim goatee, Yang had the intensity and intelligence of a real general, and the hard cold eyes of a genuine sociopath.

Half an hour later, Yang was studying a map at his desk in the strategy room he'd had equipped within the crumbling Ming temple, a large banner with the three-dragon emblem draped behind him. Through a ruined doorway, an officer entered, but not just any officer: a beautiful woman, who made the crisp gray uniform, black-leather-trimmed cap and black leather boots seem fashionable.

And not just any beautiful woman, either, but Choi, the scar-faced beauty who had positioned herself in a dark alley across from the Imhotep's nightclub to gather intelligence on Alex, Rick and Evelyn O'Connell.

She was here to report on her spy duties, standing before the desk and giving a razor-sharp salute before saying in Mandarin, *"The O'Connells are indeed in Shanghai."*

"The parents and the boy?"

"Yes, General. They assembled at the club owned by the O'Connell woman's brother, a fool named Jonathan Carnahan."

He gave her the cold, blank stare that was his response to good news, bad news and everything in between. *"Do they have the Eye?"*

"They do, General."

This news brought a remarkable response from the stone-faced general: a tiny, curt smile.

"Then our hour is at hand," he said. *"Call the troops to order."*

In minutes, General Yang was standing on the steps outside the crumbling temple to address his seventy-five mercenaries-turned-zealots, in perfect formation and supervised by the lovely woman with the scarred face, Colonel Choi.

His head was up, as he said in Mandarin, *"Soon all of our training, all of our sacrifice, will bear fruit."* He gestured downward. *"Out of this soil soaked with the blood of centuries, we will raise our emperor once more."*

All eyes were on the general, his men as motionless as the Emperor's terra-cotta warriors.

Yang continued: *"We will* live *for him . . . and die for him . . . until China is again the most powerful nation on earth, as it was two thousand years ago. We will fulfill the vision of Er Shi Huangdi and rule the world."* His eyes traveled along the rows of soldiers. *"Tonight, we few will summon the might. Tonight, our great battle begins!"*

Choi nodded permission to the troops to respond, and they did, cheering wildly and firing their weapons in the air in the ecstasy known only by true fanatics.

Neons of blue and orange and yellow and white were further illuminated by bursts of firecrackers and small rockets as the white Bentley—Jonathan Carnahan's prized possession—crawled in heavy traffic down a major Shanghai thoroughfare.

The cars were mostly American, but this traffic consisted of both tourists and natives, and was more than automotive: bicycles and rickshaws and horse-drawn wagons mingled with revelers on foot, who claimed the rain-slicked street on this New Year's Eve as their own.

Rick O'Connell rode shotgun as Jonathan drove, if this snail's pace could be calling "driving," and Alex and Evelyn were in the back. The little group was spruced up even beyond the fancy attire of the night before at Imhotep's: O'Connell and Jonathan in black tie, Alex in a white dinner jacket, Evy in a pink backless satin grown with lush white furs wrapped around her shoulders.

O'Connell watched as a rickshaw, drawn by a wrinkled prune of a man, passed them by. "We'd do better if we hired *him*," O'Connell said with a nod to the old boy.

Jonathan was smiling, though, casual at the wheel. "Chinese New Year—you have to love it."

"No," O'Connell said, "I don't."

But Jonathan, beaming, burbled blithely on. "God, I adore this country—they have all these extra holidays and drinking is virtually *mandatory* . . . a bar owner's dream!"

In the rearview mirror, O'Connell saw Evy reaching to take her son's hand, but the father's eyes caught the mother's and warned her not to. Alex was in no frame of mind to be coddled, and O'Connell knew it, and Evy got the point—she withdrew her gloved hand.

But she couldn't contain her pride in her offspring, saying to him, "I can't believe we're on our way to see your first big discovery—it's so exciting!"

Rather sullenly, as he looked out the window at the revelers and the colorful goings-on, Alex said, "After last night, I'm surprised you even want to see it at all."

Now Evy caught her husband's eyes in the rearview mirror and her look told him to say something positive to their grown-up child.

"Are you kidding, Alex?" O'Connell said. "We wouldn't miss it."

Evy smiled at him in the rearview mirror.

Then O'Connell shrugged and said, "Anyway, we have a package to drop off at the museum."

Evy frowned at him in the rearview mirror.

Alex smirked sourly. "*I* get it—*my* life and *your* mission just happen to intersect, so why not throw the kid a bone?"

O'Connell sought Evy's eyes again and saw his wife was rolling them in "Oh, brother" mode. He had once again stuck his foot in it. . . .

"Son, that's not what I meant. . . ."

Jonathan, who was more attuned to this conflict than he let on, changed the subject. "Listen, I'll pick you up in an hour and we'll go out and celebrate the New Year in style. What do you say?"

Evelyn frowned at the back of her brother's head. "Aren't you going, Jonathan?"

"My dear darling sister, I have seen enough mummies to last a lifetime. Make that a thousand lifetimes. And besides . . ." He nodded to the left. ". . . my favorite watering hole in Shanghai is just around the corner."

O'Connell made a face at his brother-in-law. "Jonathan, you already own your own bar."

"Ah yes," Jonathan said, pulling in at the portico of the massive museum, whose lights were mostly off, "but what fun is it running up a tab on yourself?"

Soon, Alex had led his parents into the rotunda of the museum, where the formality of the marble floor and massive, arched stained-glass windows were at odds with the work in progress. Crates of artifacts were stacked against the walls, and repair scaffolding lined either side of the vast chamber; a desk, presumably Roger Wilson's, was scattered with books and other research materials.

The Emperor's memorial, discovered in the crypt of the tomb, resided under worklights in the midst of the rotunda, scaffolding forming an L around the monument's platform. Almost as attuned to museum restoration as his highly trained wife, O'Connell could tell that the chariot, horses and cortege wagon—as well as the bronze statue of the Emperor himself—

had been cleaned up considerably since his son dis-covered them.

Alex pointed. "There he is—Er Shi Huangdi him-self."

"They say," O'Connell said, "that he was one evil son of a bitch."

Evy said, "Rick!" But she didn't disagree.

The three O'Connells strolled along the cortege wagon and chariot, taking it all in, and settled in front of the bronze steeds. Evy's eyes were wide in a mix-ture of parental pride and historian's interest. O'Con-nell, however, had an odd tingling feeling at the back of his neck, probably due to their proximity to a mummy, even if it was Chinese and not Egyptian.

"Very impressive," Evy said. She turned to her son, but she seemed like the youthful one, asking, "When do you get to open the sarcophagus?"

Alex grinned. "After the official red tape has been cut. I can hardly wait."

O'Connell smirked. "The phrase *rest in peace* never really took with you two, did it?"

They ignored him, Alex asking his mother, "So why don't you stick around for the next few days? We can open the Emperor's box up together . . . unless you have to get back to your new book."

She smiled wryly. "I would grasp at *any* excuse not to get back to my new book . . . but even without the benefit of avoiding work, I would like that very much. Very much indeed."

That obviously pleased Alex.

O'Connell said, "Son, would you mind tracking down Professor Wilson? And tell him we're here."

"Sure," Alex said. "No problem." Then he lifted an eyebrow and a forefinger at the bronze statue of the Emperor, then brought it over to the coffin. "Just don't wake the old fella up while I'm gone. I know what you two are *capable* of. . . ."

Alex headed out, and Evy gave her husband a sharp look that meant *Say something!*

So he did: "Hey, uh, Alex?"

Alex turned. "Yes, Dad?"

O'Connell patted the bronze rear end of the steed nearest him; he nodded toward the sarcophagus and the rest of the magnificent find. "This sure is something."

Alex just stared at him.

"Big stuff," O'Connell said awkwardly.

"Right, Dad. Whatever you say."

And the boy went off.

Alex was moving through the darkened hallway of the closed museum when he sensed something, and turned quickly, but saw nothing. Something familiar tickled his nostrils. A scent . . . what was that? Perfume? Where might he have smelled it before?

He shrugged and moved on.

He had not seen the shadowy form duck back into an alcove as he walked by, unaware he had passed the catlike female adversary with whom he'd tangled at the tomb of Er Shi Huangdi.

Back in the rotunda, O'Connell had removed the Eye of Shambhala from its box and was presently idly bouncing the precious chunk of blue diamond in its oversized gold-snake setting in his palm as if the priceless artifact were a baseball. He was studying Evy as she studied the monument admiringly. Again, her pride in her son was evident; but so was her interest as an archaeologist and curator.

Something else was evident: his wife was ravishingly beautiful tonight, in the slinky backless satin gown and the white furs. Funny how a guy could lose track of things like that. . . .

He said, "You know, you have a special glow tonight. I haven't seen you light up like this for a long time."

She blushed—actually blushed! He felt good that he still could have that kind of effect on her.

She said, "I guess maybe mummies bring out the young girl in me."

Their eyes met and their hands did, too, but the moment was interrupted by a voice from behind them: "Did you two take a wrong turn at Cairo?"

They spun to see their old friend Roger Wilson, looking distinguished in a dark suit and bow tie; what little was left of his white hair was brushed back. To O'Connell, seeing his old friend all gussied up seemed quite at odds with his memory of the dusty, disheveled figure who had worked at his side on numerous digs.

"Roger," Evelyn said warmly.

"Wilson," O'Connell said, with a little edge, since this was after all the bad influence who had wooed Alex away from Harvard.

"Sorry to interrupt, Richard, Evelyn," Wilson said with a smile.

"When Alex told me you'd gone legit," O'Connell said, "I could hardly believe it. What's this 'Professor' stuff, anyway?"

Wilson shrugged. "Eminently respectable, that's me—still pillaging tombs, only now in the name of preservation. I'm curator here, and a visiting lecturer at any number of colleges and universities."

O'Connell smirked. "Don't remind me."

Evy gestured to the sarcophagus on the chariot and said, "Congratulations on your latest discovery."

Wilson waved a hand. "Alex deserves the lion's share of credit. Hell of a lad you have there, Richard. He's like the son I never had."

"Well," O'Connell said, hands on hips, "he's also the only son we *ever* had, so the next time you want to go globe-trotting with him, give us a heads-up first, okay?"

"Of course." Wilson folded his hands before a fairly ample middle mound. "Now, I believe you have something that belongs to the museum. . . ."

O'Connell hefted the Eye playfully, then handed it

over to the curator. Wilson did not bounce the Eye of Shangri-la in his palm, rather held it there like the priceless treasure it was.

"I knew I could count on you two," he said.

O'Connell frowned. Now it was Wilson who had an edge in his voice, and that odd tingling was back. . . .

From the shadows emerged two figures in gray military garb, both with blouses bearing odd three-headed-dragon insignias: a tall woman, lovely but with one cheek scarred, and a slender, dead-eyed, slightly shorter individual who carried himself with cold confidence.

With the hand that did not bear the Eye, Wilson gestured presentationally. "Rick, Evelyn—I'd like you to meet my good friends—General Yang and Colonel Choi."

"A pleasure to meet such celebrated adventurers," Yang said, with the tiniest of bows. "But I'm afraid your work, Mr. O'Connell, Mrs. O'Connell . . . is not quite done."

Both O'Connells wheeled toward their old friend, who produced a Colt 1911 as magically as Bugs Bunny does a carrot.

Evelyn, shocked and disappointed, said, "Roger! What on earth is the meaning of this?"

O'Connell said nothing, way ahead of his wife, for once.

Wilson, with a smile that was almost as dead as General Yang's eyes, pointed the weapon their way and said, "You have General Yang to thank for your son's success. He's the one who financed Alex's dig. We're all in this together, cheek by jowl."

Wilson edged over to Yang and handed him the Eye.

"So you set us up, huh, Roger?" O'Connell said. "With friends like you, who needs betraying bastards?"

"Now, Richard," Wilson said. "We're neither one of us angels."

"*You* may be soon," O'Connell said, "but I wouldn't count on it. You'll likely be going in the opposite direction."

With a nod at O'Connell, Yang instructed Wilson, "Search him. He's not the kind of man who goes anywhere unarmed."

Yang and the lovely, scarred colonel held their own sidearms on O'Connell as Wilson gave his old comrade a frisk. The result of the search was two .38 Smith & Wessons, from under either armpit, the curator tossing the guns across the marble floor, sending them skittering. But O'Connell noted where they'd gone. . . .

"The Eye of Shambhala," Evelyn said, "belongs to the people of China. You can't do this, Roger. You'll die in disgrace."

Wilson said nothing, continuing his frisking of his former friend, finding a set of brass knuckles in O'Connell's right-hand pocket, and plucking a butterfly knife from his waistband.

Wilson said drily, "When you dress formally, Richard, you really go all out."

"Enjoy yourself, Roger. This won't last long. So how much are Yin and Yang here paying you? What are the services of a snake running these days?"

Wilson had just discovered a snub-nosed pistol strapped to O'Connell's ankle. "Enough for me to pull some strings at the Foreign Office, and make sure you and your lovely wife were the ones chosen to deliver the Eye."

"Why us, Roger?"

But it was Yang who answered: "For one thing, Mr. O'Connell, we trusted your wife's expertise in handling such a precious artifact, and yours in protecting it. The Eye of Shangri-la, as some call it, contains the Elixir of Eternal Life. Mrs. O'Connell, I must impose upon you to open it."

Evy turned as white as her fur. Her eyes went to the sarcophagus and then back to the general in horrified realization. Taking a step back, she said, "My God, no. You . . . you mean to use it to awaken the *Emperor*, don't you?"

This time Wilson answered for the general: "Yes, indeed. But not just Er Shi Huangdi—his entire terra-cotta army." Wilson shrugged as if they were discussing the weather. "That's the general idea, at least."

O'Connell's stomach was churning. "You people don't know what you're dealing with—*we* do. You do not want to unleash this kind of thing on the world. We, all of us, narrowly escaped when Imhotep returned, *twice*—and now you want to raise the most evil Emperor of them all from the dead?"

"In a word," Yang said, "yes."

"Raising one mummy is crazy—raising an army of them is bloody insane."

O'Connell lurched toward Yang and got the barrel of Wilson's pistol across the back of his head for the trouble. While this was going on, Evy used the moment to go for the knife in the sheath on her thigh— no one had bothered to frisk her—but the big scar-faced beauty in the gray uniform was suddenly behind her, wresting the blade from Evy's grasp.

Yang shoved the groggy O'Connell toward the steps of the scaffolding.

Wilson said, "Easy there, Richard. Time to open up the sarcophagus and wake our sleeping friend."

Yang had moved close to Evy and now held the precious gem with its golden-snakes setting out to her; on the golden oval base from which the snakes arose were etched letters in ancient Mandarin.

"*Read* it," the general demanded. "Read the inscription—*now*."

Elsewhere in the Shanghai Museum, Alex came up behind the lithe figure in black, who was moving along the arcade windows, looking down through them at the rotunda below.

He said, "You never called. I thought our first date went really well."

She spun to him, eyes flashing. "There's no time for games, Alex."

He grinned at her. "You know my name, but I don't know yours. That's not fair."

"It's Lin."

"Short but sweet. So, Lin, care to explain why you tried to kill me?"

"I could," she said, gesturing to the windows with a view on the room below. "Or we could save your parents. I'll leave it up to you."

He smirked at her, hands on his hips. "Right. Nice try. I go over and take a look, and you kick my ass through the window."

She gazed at him as blank as a Buddha. "See for yourself."

Something about her tone convinced him, and he cautiously moved to where he could see through the second-story window . . .

. . . and looked down at Professor Wilson using a handgun to move Alex's father toward the scaffolding while two military types, a man and a woman, trained guns on Alex's mother.

Wilson's bitter betrayal was immediately evident, and Alex muttered, "The son of a bitch . . ."

"You can whine," she said. "Or we can do something about it. Your choice."

Up on the monument's platform, Wilson was prodding O'Connell toward the sarcophagus, while on the

101

marble floor below, General Yang faced Evy, who held the Eye in her palms as she studied the inscription etched in the gold oval from which the golden snakes rose to grip the precious stone.

"I'm afraid," she said, "ancient Chinese is not my strong suit. . . ."

"Perhaps you need some encouragement. Wilson!"

Wilson looked at Yang, who nodded, and the curator thumbed back the hammer on the pistol and aimed the weapon at O'Connell's heart. "Sorry, Richard."

O'Connell said, "No you aren't."

"Stop!" Evy cried. "I'll *do* it. I *can* read it. Just leave my husband alone."

O'Connell was shaking his head. "Evy, don't be a fool—they're going to kill me anyway. Don't do it!"

Her glance up at him held many things—anguish, love, regret, but perhaps most of all knowledge of what turning loose another reanimated madman would mean to the world. . . .

But O'Connell could see that the world was something his wife was willing to trade for her husband's life; and wouldn't he have done the same for her?

She said, "The inscription says that only a drop of blood from a person pure of heart can open the Eye. I'm afraid you need a virgin for that, and looking around the room, I would say we are in rather short supply of those."

General Yang's small smile was enormously vile.

"Your husband was right, Mrs. O'Connell. I *do* intend to kill him anyway."

And the general trained the weapon on O'Connell, up on the monument.

Evy thrust herself between the general's weapon and her husband, putting herself at point-blank range. "No! I did as you said, I read you the bloody thing, don't *do* it!"

Yang lowered the gun and smiled. "The inscription, as I interpret it, Mrs. O'Connell, does not require a virgin. But it does require someone pure of heart. And only the pure of heart would sacrifice himself . . . or *her*self . . . for the one she loves."

Colonel Choi, summoned by Yang's sideways glance, came over and, with sensual grace, removed the glove from Evy's right hand; then Choi unsheathed a knife and extended its blade over Evy's pink upturned palm.

Yang snapped to Wilson, "*Open* it!"

Up on the platform, Wilson cautiously lifted a crowbar that leaned against the scaffolding rail and handed the tool to O'Connell, who went quickly to work prying the lid from the sarcophagus, creating a nails-on-blackboard grinding that filled the rotunda.

The grinding masked any sound from above—though that sound was nearly nonexistent already—as Lin, followed by Alex, climbed down onto the scaffolding, hidden from view by piles of brick and other building materials, block and tackles swagged from the corners of the chamber.

When their worst suspicions were confirmed by the sight of General Yang and Colonel Choi, both facing Alex's mother, who was passing her hand over the Eye, held out in the general's paired palms, the two exchanged glances of alarm.

Lin thought, *The Eye of Shambhala*, Alex thinking the same, but substituting *Shangri-la*.

With the point of her knife, the cruelly lovely Choi pricked Evy's finger and a few drops of pure-of-heart blood dripped down into the fabled object held in the general's cupped palms, blood like red mercury gliding over and down and around and through the mesh of golden snakes.

Evy's eyes widened, as—incredibly—the stone appeared to absorb her blood.

Then, as a few drops touched the inscription oval, the decorative snakes seemed to come alive and writhe and wriggle and release themselves from the grip of the gem they had enshrouded for countless centuries.

And now the gem itself began to transform: the diamond split along its facet lines, the golden lattice around it now wholly unfurled, lotuslike, and within crystalline petals sat a stamen floating in a substance that could only be liquid diamond—the Elixir of Eternal Life!

This magical metamorphosis had taken place in the upturned palms of that self-styled warlord, that most unmagical General Yang, whose usually stoic expression had also transformed—into one of child-like awe.

Wilson—knowing both O'Connells were dangerous and that the longer this took, the riskier it was—frowned down from the monument and demanded, "Yang! Get on with it!"

Throughout, O'Connell had been both watching and working, gouging that crowbar in under the sarcophagus lid and prying with all his strength, always looking for a moment he could take advantage of. But that moment refused to come and, now, furious with his own helplessness, he shoved the ajar lid with savage abandon and the thing crashed to the monument floor.

The thunderclap of that brought Yang back to reality, or at least his concept of it, and with the blossomed Eye in one hand now, he climbed the stairs onto the platform. Below, Evy remained at knifepoint in Choi's custody.

Referring to the liquid-diamond Elixir, Yang spoke with more emotion than might be thought possible from such a man: "Once this touches the lips of Er Shi Huangdi, the Emperor will not merely once again walk among us—he will be *immortal*!"

O'Connell was between Yang and the opened sarcophagus, the skeleton revealed there, in weathered royal robes and with a golden medallion at its neck.

The general snarled, *"Move back! . . .* Wilson, dispense with this fool."

Wilson, with perhaps the tiniest smirk of regret, swung the Colt automatic into position and was about to squeeze the trigger when someone kicked the curator in the head . . . *from above.*

O'Connell had just witnessed an amazing sight: his son, Alex, his formal white coat abandoned somewhere, swinging down from the right rear corner of the rotunda, swooping in from a block-and-tackle swag!

And then, with timing that could not have been improved upon had the two young rescuers been through weeks of training, Lin launched herself similarly from the left rear corner, swinging down on her own rope, and her feet slammed into Yang, smashing him hard into the rear of the monument, against the bronze chariot, the Elixir splashing onto the bronze armor of the statue of the Emperor at the reins of the bronze horses.

And that Elixir was absorbed within the bronze armor, much as Evelyn O'Connell's blood had been into the Eye of Shangri-la.

Using the edge of the chariot, O'Connell launched himself, making a spectacular gymnastic vault to the museum's marble floor, then went sliding toward his discarded guns.

In the meantime, Lin had landed, catlike, withdrawing the dragon dagger, and then she did something that

106

would have seemed very peculiar to those around her, had they not been otherwise occupied: with a graceful martial-arts pirouette, she came around to slam that dagger down into the open coffin and deep into the chest of the skeleton within.

Something significant that would have meant nothing to the others had they noticed—with the possible exception of archaeologist Evelyn O'Connell—caused Lin's dismayed expression when she came face-to-face with a gold medallion around the neck of the skeletal remains.

Lin recognized the medallion as that of the Emperor's chief eunuch and head minister, Li Zhou, and knew at once something was terribly wrong . . .

. . . *because this skeleton was almost certainly not the Emperor's*.

Choi had turned away from Evelyn and was poised to throw her knife at O'Connell when Evy shoved the woman's arm and the knife flew harmlessly from the colonel's grasp, clattering onto the marble.

Furious, Choi faced Evy, and the woman in the gray uniform with black-leather trappings crouched into a posture that spoke of an imminent martial-arts attack. . . .

What Choi did not know was that Evy had been, in another life long ago, the Princess Nefertiti, and was skilled in ancient methods of combat not usually found in former librarians. Plus, her husband had taught her a trick or two.

So when the two women traded martial-arts blows, fists, arms, legs, blurring in motion, Choi was surprised by her opponent's quickness, dexterity and skill.

But Evy remained modest: "I must warn you, I'm a trifle rusty. . . ."

The rust got shaken off quickly, however, as the two women went at it, Choi's cap flying off and Evy's hair coming undone, her furs flying. Finally Evy grabbed on to the taller woman and took her for a ride in a back roll that sent the colonel crashing into a pile of crates.

And Colonel Choi apparently needed a breather, because she did not get up.

Evy, frankly impressed with herself, thought, *Not bad, old girl, not bad.*

On the monument platform, their old "friend" Wilson was trying to get to his feet but Alex stopped that, kicking a gun from his mentor's hand, popping it up so that the boy could catch it. Then he gave Wilson another swift kick in the head, which sent the professor napping.

Nearby, Lin was ripping the medallion from the skeleton's neck. Her eyes and nostrils flared. "It's a decoy—this is *not* Er Shi Huangdi!"

Alex came over for a look. "Who the hell is it, then?"

"I believe it is his head minister. I have seen pictures of the symbol on that medallion."

"Okay, then where the hell's your emperor?"

"He is not *my* emperor!"

This discussion was interrupted by the sound of a horse whinnying. Both Alex and Lin turned to frown at the bizarre sight of a bronze hoof pawing the platform's floor. And then all of the legs of the horses were alive, the animals shifting in place, bronze manes shaking, as the entire rotunda began to tremble and the trembling turned to tremors and it was as if an earthquake had selected this one chamber in Shanghai in which to do all its destructive work. . . .

Lin dove from the platform and rolled to a corner of the rotunda while Alex did the same, moving to the opposite corner, both covering up instinctively, which was fortunate, because the "statue" of the Emperor blasted apart, chunks of bronze flying, revealing a second, slightly smaller statue hidden within, like one Russian doll in another.

O'Connell dove for cover, too, as did Evy. He had his guns now, two of them anyway, one for either hand, and was getting to his feet when out of the dustcloud aftermath of the explosion appeared a terracotta figure, its arms raised as if in pain, or perhaps rage.

And Emperor Er Shi Huangdi took his first breath in two millennia.

Rick O'Connell, his hair mussed, his tuxedo powdered with dust, his face dirty, had an expression that might have been a smile but really wasn't, not if you studied the dread that mingled with resolve in his unblinking blue eyes.

"Here we go again," he breathed.

And on the floor nearby, Evy O'Connell—seeing the reddish-brown terra-cotta Emperor alive up on his chariot with his impatient steeds awaiting him to take rein—was thinking the very same thing.

·❦ 5 ❧·

Shanghaied

Emperor Er Shi Huangdi, awakening to find himself a terra-cotta figure standing in a chariot, before bronze steeds restlessly come to life, was welcomed to the twentieth century by General Yang, who stood on the monument platform nearby.

Head bowed, the general spoke in ancient Mandarin: *"I have awakened you, my lord. I live to serve you, and to attend to your final transformation. Allow me please to guide you to a safe haven."*

The Emperor's nod was barely discernible but enough to encourage Yang to climb up onto the chariot.

No sooner had the general done so than the revived Emperor Mummy snatched up the reins and began to whip his bronze steeds. The entire chariot and the cortege wagon it drew lurched forward, then plunged off the platform and, building speed, began to lumber across the marble floor of the rotunda, bound for the huge stained-glass window directly ahead.

Rick O'Connell, a .38 Smith & Wesson revolver in either hand, raced after the two-sectioned vehicle, unloading on the hard-clay Emperor Mummy and his passenger, the sharp cracks of the handguns punctuating the sound of the galloping hooves and rumbling chariot wheels like Chinese New Year's firecrackers, and having about as much impact.

Not so much to his astonishment as to his dismay, O'Connell—perhaps the most seasoned mummy fighter on the planet—watched as a bullet chipped off the Emperor's ear, only for that ear to spontaneously regenerate.

Bastard's impervious, O'Connell thought.

Unfortunately none of his shots claimed the not-impervious Yang, who was firing back with his own pistol at the pursuing O'Connell, driving him back behind a pillar as building materials in the path of the chariot were churned to debris and scattered, chunks of God-knew-what going every which way.

In the meantime, another player was running after the chariot, attempting to hitch a ride.

Roger Wilson, his tuxedo dust-splotched now, had a look of utter frustration as he pursued his ride to fame and fortune, yelling, "Wait for me! Wait for *me* . . . !"

And O'Connell had to admit the old SOB, for his age and weight, ran quickly, even managing to make his way up alongside the terra-cotta Emperor as the chariot built speed going toward the big rotunda window. Wilson was trying to clamber up onto the vehicle, next to Er Shi Huangdi, who reacted harshly. In the Emperor Mummy's defense, he had no reason to recognize Wilson as an ally, just some wayward hitchhiker.

That was scant solace for Wilson, as the Emperor Mummy unsheathed his sword and swung it with a *whoosh*, neatly taking Wilson's head off and sending it rolling into the periphery with the other rubble, the professor's headless body stumbling along a step or two before collapsing in a pile that even the Eye of Shangri-la could not do anything for.

As O'Connell, from behind his pillar, threw gunfire at Yang, who threw gunfire back, son Alex was dashing at the chariot from the other side, using the distraction his father was providing to slide as if into home plate, right underneath the rumbling wagon, where he grabbed brackets on the undercarriage of the cortege wagon and got purchase.

Unlike Wilson, Alex had successfully hitched a ride.

Lin had watched Alex's move and now imitated it, the lithe female warrior in black similarly sliding, and with a hand Alex helped her get a hold under the chariot as it continued to gather speed.

Both Alex and Lin held on for dear life as the four bronze horses burst through the window in a spray of shattering glass, bearing the chariot and cortege wagon from the first-floor rotunda into the Shanghai night.

Within moments the metallic steeds were smashing through the museum's wrought-iron rear gates, and then the Emperor's chariot thundered onto the nearby city street, even as Alex and Lin hung on below the attached cortege wagon, every bone in their bodies, every tooth in their mouths, getting rattled like dice.

The Emperor Mummy proceeded to welcome in the New Year as his chariot hurtled down a street festooned with Chinese lanterns and beautiful flowers, the unlikely vehicle disrupting everything in its path, including the festive atmosphere. Revelers, rickshaws, bicycles, all did their best to get out of the way and, when they couldn't, were smashed aside. Market stalls were knocked apart while celebrants both tourist and local went scrambling in dumbfounded fear. One crushed bicycle seemed to reach out for Alex and Lin, catching the young woman's black coat and ripping away its lower half.

Back at the museum, O'Connell and Evy were running out through those wrecked rear gates just as a truck—whose canvas side panels proclaimed TSE KAR WAIT FIREWORKS COMPANY—was rumbling by. O'Connell, a revolver in either hand, tried to wave the driver down, but the vehicle barreled on, the driver either not hearing . . . or perhaps spotting O'Connell's weapons. . . .

114

The couple, whose evening wear was soiled and ripped already, went sprinting after the slow-moving vehicle and jumped onto its running boards, on either side, in near unison.

The Chinese driver began to curse at them. To O'Connell this was just singsong gibberish and, anyway, he had no time for discussion in any language.

"Sorry, pal," O'Connell said. "Mummy on the loose . . ."

And that was all the explanation the driver got before O'Connell opened the truck door, yanked the guy out from behind the wheel and dropped him unceremoniously off on the pavement. More cursing, more gibberish followed, but only for a moment. The truck commandeered, Evy was behind the wheel now and O'Connell was riding shotgun, or anyway Smith & Wesson revolver. . . .

A few blocks away, Jonathan Carnahan was emerging from the Jolin Bar, his favorite gin mill (other than his own), bidding several Chinese regulars a fond good-bye. He spoke to them in Mandarin and was quite proud of being able to do so, unaware of how terrible he was at it: *"Gong xi fa chai cha cha. . . ."*

Knowing he was going to be driving, Jonathan had held it down to just one cocktail—well, two. So he was feeling singularly sober, and pleased with himself for being so, when a chariot drawn by horses of bronze, commanded by what appeared to be a reddish-brown living statue, and hauling some sort of wagon, came careening around the corner a block down.

Jonathan, in the process of unlocking the door of his prized Bentley, parked on the street, knew damned well this was no hallucination, because he— like the O'Connells—was one of a rare breed of human being: his experiences in Egypt had led him not to be surprised when a mummy decided to get itself reanimated.

This did not prevent him from blurting in dismay, "No! *No!* Bloody hell! *Bloody* fuh . . ."

The rest of his remark was blotted out by a tram rumbling by that also served to narrow the street and send the oncoming chariot veering toward Jonathan, and his parked vehicle.

"Hey!" Jonathan shouted. "You there—watch where you're driving that thing!"

The Emperor Mummy did not seem to hear, or anyway care, and the pounding bronze hoofbeats grew louder as the strange procession bore down on Jonathan, and the bizarre vehicle was only half a length away when Jonathan dove over the hood of his Bentley. He landed on the sidewalk in a heap just as the chariot sideswiped the love of his life, then added insult to injury—actually, injury to injury—when the spikes on the cortege wagon wheels blew out both his tires and ripped a wide gash in the Bentley's sheet metal.

The chariot rumbled off and Jonathan got to his

feet and examined the damage. He was almost in tears, and trembling, not in fear, but in rage. He was swearing revenge when a fireworks truck pulled up and slowed and a knife blade from within the rear of the vehicle split the canvas side and O'Connell stuck his head out.

"Climb aboard, Jonathan! We have work to do!"

Jonathan allowed himself to be hauled aboard, shaking his head, saying, "Honestly, the two of you—you're virtually *mummy* magnets, aren't you?"

Up front, Evy accelerated.

A block away, the chariot was on Main Street, plowing wildly down the broad avenue, crushing anything unfortunate enough to be in its path. Underneath the rough-riding cart, Alex and Lin were working to move, from handhold to handhold, to the rear of the cortege wagon. Right now they were almost to the back bumpers. They were unaware that Alex's parents were at all in pursuit, much less in a fireworks truck some hundred yards back, and closing.

In the rear of the truck, O'Connell was ripping canvas away so that he and Jonathan could get a view over the cab. Jonathan had discovered a big red rocket that might have been the mother of all the fireworks crated and piled back there. The two men lifted the thing up and onto the roof of the cab. Evy flinched a little as she heard them slam the rocket down, not aware of what her husband and brother were up to.

Right now O'Connell was explaining the situation

to Jonathan as wind whipped their hair and they bounced up and down with the jostle of the truck, from which Evy was coaxing considerable speed.

"We're only going to get one shot at this, Jon," he said. Then to Evy in the cab, he shouted, "Honey! Drive *nice* and *straight*!"

Then to Jonathan, he said, "Okay, buddy—light 'er up!"

Jonathan nodded and, thinking of his Bentley and the horrendous gash in its poor side, he thumbed his gold-plated Dunhill lighter and held the flame to the fuse. Then he stuck his fingers in his ears.

O'Connell grinned at his brother-in-law. "Happy New Year."

Then the rocket took off, and its blastoff almost blew the two men out and off the back of the truck.

Down the street the rocket screamed, O'Connell's aim dead-on. Half a moment before what would have been a direct hit, the Emperor Mummy turned unblinking dead eyes to see the rocket coming and, with a simple gesture of his head, redirected the spark-spewing missile and sent it instead into an electric trolley car.

The force of the explosion threw the trolley, like a toy train, into the air, passengers diving off as the car and the blast shattered neon signs and ripped wooden signs off structures. The Emperor Mummy guided his bronze steeds deftly around the resulting rubble.

Even a seasoned mummy fighter like Rick O'Con-

nell could hardly have known that Er Shi Huangdi possessed a mastery of fire.

And even if he had known, O'Connell had another crisis, albeit a small one, on his hands: the launch of the rocket had somehow set the seat of Jonathan's pants on fire. O'Connell began smacking the flames with his hands.

Jonathan, unaware his ass was on fire, objected: "Stop that! Why in bloody hell are you smacking me on the bum?"

"Because your bum is on fire!"

"On fire? Well then, crikey, man, smack it! *Smack it!*"

But smacking wasn't doing the trick, so O'Connell yanked off his dinner jacket and roughly smothered the flames attacking his brother-in-law's behind. "Stay still!"

"You stay still, with a flaming ass!"

"Hold on, it—it's *almost* out. . . . It's out."

Chin up, his dignity as shredded as the seat of his pants, Jonathan said, "Would you do me a favor, dear brother-in-law? Next time you're in Shanghai, will you give me sufficient warning so that I might be the hell *elsewhere*?"

"You're welcome."

Then the two men almost lost their balance as Evy hung a wicked left, clipping the curb. Up ahead, fires raged in the wake of the trolley mishap.

O'Connell leaned down to call through the rear

window into the cab. "Evy! Sweetie!" He pointed. "The mummy went *that* way. . . ."

She called, "I'm taking a shortcut!"

Meanwhile, Alex had helped Lin up and over the back bumpers onto the cortege wagon, where they hunkered down at the foot of the sarcophagus that separated them from the chariot and Er Shi Huangdi and General Yang. The pounding hoofbeats and the rumble over cobblestones gave them cover to whisper, as they assessed their situation.

Alex handed Lin his pistol. "Cover me. I'll go after the Emperor—take him by surprise."

She handed the weapon back. "No, *I'll* go after the Emperor."

He grinned at her. "Trust me—I'm pretty sure I have more experience with mummies than you do."

His light brown hair was an unruly mess and his face was smudged here and there, but he looked very good to Lin, who found herself enormously attracted to this young man.

But she insisted. "I have to do it—I have the only weapon that can kill him."

Her eyes said she meant business. And, truth be told, after fighting with her, Alex was convinced she could take care of herself, even if he wouldn't have minded doing the job for her.

So he said, "Okay, Lin—you win. *This* time."

Back on the fireworks truck, Alex's father was in

the hands of another strong woman—Alex's mother—who was demonstrating exactly what her "shortcut" was: the truck plowed through the brick wall of a Buddhist temple, scattering worshippers celebrating the New Year, and driving diagonally across its courtyard. This caused chaos in the temple, of course, knocking over incense stalls and malla-bead vendors, with more than one chicken squawking and wing-flapping its displeasure as Evy pounded through.

O'Connell and Jonathan, holding on for this thrill ride, had figured they'd experienced the worst, and then Evy burst through another brick wall. Jonathan was launched backward but not out of the truck, fortunately hitting a metal strut and settling down for a knocked-cold nap.

O'Connell, about to scream at his wife, stifled it because, sure enough, they now *bump-bump-bump*ed through the brick rubble onto Olympic Street, where the chariot was racing toward them, so close that the Emperor Mummy had to rein his horses to keep the chariot from colliding with Evy, who had pulled in front of him. As Er Shi Huangdi tried to steer around her, Evy swerved and stayed out in front.

Er Shi Huangdi shot a fierce glance at General Yang, and commanded in ancient Mandarin, *"Clear them from my path!"*

Yang immediately began to open fire on the truck.

O'Connell pushed Jonathan into a relatively safe

position, then went over and lowered the truck's tail-gate, and almost tumbled out, since Evy had just swerved to avoid Yang's slugs.

He scrambled back up to lean through the cab window and hand Evy one of the Smith & Wesson revolvers.

"You might need this," he said.

Then he leaned in some more and kissed her on the back of the neck. She smiled. She seemed to feel the old tingle—he certainly did.

Her eyes flicked from the road to his. "Where are you going?"

"Out. Don't wait up."

Then he sprinted toward the rear of the truck, where the chariot was close behind now, and leaped!

O'Connell reached out and grabbed one of the bronze horses storming toward him, its nostrils flaring, and got it by its pounding neck and held precariously on, riding backward and upside down, the cool feel of the bronze on his palms strange in contrast to the hot breath of the steed.

Back on the truck, Jonathan came to. He made his way up and crawled in through the window into the cab and sat beside his sister. "Where's Rick?"

"Where do you suppose?"

Jonathan looked back, and saw O'Connell struggling like a drunken Cossack trying to hold on to that bronze horse. "Oh dear . . ."

But finally O'Connell hauled himself up onto the

horse's back and, like a cowboy chased by Indians, began throwing shots behind him. Again, one of his bullets caught the Emperor Mummy's ear, blowing it off . . .

. . . and again it regenerated in an instant.

"Kill him!" demanded Er Shi Huangdi.

The chariot plowed through a sidewalk café, scattering partygoers and demolishing tables, the rough ride making Yang's shots go wild.

O'Connell flicked out his butterfly knife to see if he could sever the bronze harness keeping the steeds together; to his relief, the bronze cut like leather, and within moments O'Connell was able to rein his horse and had soon dropped back to the rear of the cortege, where Alex and Lin were behind the sarcophagus, about to make their move.

O'Connell held his hand out to his son. "Come on, Alex! *Jump!*"

As Alex signaled his father to back away, Lin said with a smirk, "Well, so much for our surprise . . ."

Alex's eyebrows were up. "What can I say? The old man has a hero complex."

And as Lin feared, Yang now realized the wagon behind the chariot bore other passengers. He turned and fired at Alex, who ducked down behind the sarcophagus for cover, returning fire.

Yang ducked behind the skirts of the chariot as Alex's slugs pinged off their thick bronze.

With the general busy with their stowaways, the

Emperor Mummy was left by himself to deal with O'Connell and the now stray bronze horse. The Emperor locked eyes with the metal steed and the animal went out of control, bucking and veering off and down a narrow alley.

O'Connell, with no idea why the horse had spooked, yelled, "Whoa!" to no avail, as the thing kept bucking and he kept slamming back down on its bare bronze back.

And, once again, seasoned mummy fighter Rick O'Connell could not know that Er Shi Huangdi had a mastery over metal.

The other end of the alleyway O'Connell was unwillingly racing down was Warehouse Street. Here hogsheads of Tsingtao Beer were being craned in a cargo net across the street to a waiting flatbed truck. The runaway horse, with O'Connell on its back, dashed down the narrow alleyway, the crane swinging into view and blocking passage.

O'Connell dropped below the withers, hoping to avoid collision, but the horse plowed right through the crane and its bronze head, in a shower of sparks, was sheared clean off. The detached horse's head landed in the lap of an old Chinese wino, sleeping off an early start to the New Year under a tattered blanket, only to wake up with a scream.

O'Connell grabbed the reins of the headless horse, but trying to steer the blind creature was a pointless process, and the best he could do was grab the mane and the jagged hollow neck and hold on. . . .

Throughout all this, Evy had managed to stay in front of the chariot and keep the Emperor pinned behind her, maneuvering as necessary.

This infuriated the Emperor Mummy, who could see beyond the truck to where Annie Avenue widened into a square. To Yang he said, *"Use your weapon on the fire sticks."*

Driving his remaining horses, the Emperor managed to pull the chariot abreast of the truck as Yang pumped rounds into the canvas-lined rear of the vehicle, more sharp cracks rising above the hoofbeats and chariot wheels and engine noise. Several of Yang's bullets pierced wooden firecracker crates riding behind Evy, and set off a chain reaction, a blazing, noisy fireworks show suddenly exploding through the truck's canvas roof.

Evy, unable to control the truck, rocked by the ongoing blasts, veered onto Warehouse Street, and the chariot pulled away, going down Lantern Street.

Yang's attention drawn away from them, Alex and Lin, hunkered at the foot of the sarcophagus, faced each other.

Alex said, "I'll lay down cover. You go up and over. Ready?"

She nodded.

The chariot barreled around the next curve, going

past the front museum gates as the chase came back to nearly square one. Once again the Emperor Mummy and his chariot were on Main Street, now traveling east to west.

Alex began laying down fire with his revolver and Yang ducked for cover while Lin dropped into the sarcophagus. She crawled over Li Zhou's bones, edging toward the chariot and the Emperor, her dragon dagger at the ready. Popping up, ready to strike, Lin found herself facing Yang, who shot her twice at nearly point-blank range, blowing her back into the box.

Alex screamed: "Lin!"

Er Shi Huangdi guided his rig over a high curb and sent the distracted Alex catapulting off the rear of the chariot; he hit the pavement, hard, but reached up and grabbed the wagon's black cleat, one-handed, his gun gone. Now he was being dragged. . . .

Within the sarcophagus, the young female who'd suffered two wounds was not dead; she was waiting for her two wounds to regenerate, much as the Emperor Mummy's terra-cotta ears had reappeared. As the bullet punctures resealed, leaving her completely healed, she was relieved that Alex had not witnessed this outright magic.

Alex, dragged but not defeated, was using a combination of sheer will and young-bull strength to latch on to another cleat, and somehow got a leg over the wagon's side, and was attempting to pull himself up when a slender hand reached down and yanked him up and onto the rear of the cart, alongside the sarcophagus.

And in fact Lin was inside that sarcophagus, leaning out to give him that helping hand.

As they bumped along, he said, "Thank God—I thought you were dead!"

"Yang missed."

Alex did not have time to contemplate how Yang might have missed at such close range, because he could see the Emperor Mummy up there, craned to send his dead eyes back their way.

Er Shi Huangdi turned to Yang and shouted, *"Release the wagon!"*

Yang quickly went to work disconnecting the linchpin between the vehicle's two halves.

Not far away, unaware of what was to come, at the Shanghai Opera's outdoor theater, a crowd of New Year's Eve theatergoers was being entertained by "The Disciples of the Pear Garden." The cast members were working themselves up to the climax of *The Nose*, a performer in a Chen Qi mask squaring off in song against another in a Chong Heihu mask.

Back on the Emperor Mummy's bronze-steed-drawn ride, Yang had pulled the pin, separating the chariot from the cortege wagon, which sent the latter into a wicked spin on its two wheels.

Alex, not wanting to be thrown off, dove into the sarcophagus with Lin. On top of her, he was about to excuse taking this liberty when the coffin was propelled by centrifugal force off the wagon and sent flying onto Billboard Street.

At the outdoor opera, more singing was under way, pleasing its audience, at least until Rick O'Connell on his headless horse burst through the rear paper gates just as the sarcophagus came sliding through the main gate.

Bailout time, O'Connell thought, and like a circus acrobat, he got up and stood on the back of the runaway horse and then leaped up for a strung banner. He was up and off the horse, which got promptly clipped by the coffin. The headless metal horse flew over Alex and Lin down in the sarcophagus like a bowling pin.

Elsewhere, Evy was coming around the bend onto Main Street and almost ran head-on into the chariot, but the Emperor Mummy avoided the out-of-control, fireworks-spewing vehicle. By now the glare in the truck cab was blinding, and then there, in front of Evy, too close to do anything about it, was the cortege wagon, spinning.

She yelled to Jonathan beside her, "Abandon ship!"

And sister jumped from one side and brother from the other, hitting the pavement, skidding on their own flesh as the truck plowed into the wagon, which exploded in a huge fireball that put a very big period on the end of the sentence of the chase.

Because the chariot, unburdened by the cortege wagon and its stowaways, driven by a statue come to life, had charged away into the neon-streaked night.

·❧ 6 ❧·

Plane Crazy

When the cab pulled up to the curb in front of the posh nitery known as Imhotep's, the distinctive neon sign was off and the uniformed doormen were nowhere to be seen. One by one, the members of the bedraggled O'Connell party emerged from the cab, their fancy evening wear ripped and filthy and scorched, their faces smudged and bruised, their hair a mess. Among them was Lin, whose cat-burglar-black attire was also shredded and soiled, in particular the coat she wore over her black top and pants, though perhaps she looked the least worse for wear.

Rick O'Connell exited last, moving slowly and wincing from the pain that bouncing on that bronze bucking bronco had caused the family jewels, which were no Eye of Shangri-la but were priceless to him. Jonathan was weaving as if drunk, though he was very much sober, having survived concussions, explosions and more. The cabbie leaned to look out the passenger window and scowl as he barked at Jonathan in Mandarin.

Jonathan, closing his eyes as if hungover, said, "Uh, Rick, my boy—the taxi fare, if you please."

O'Connell, whose tuxedo was a shredded memory, said, "Do I look like a man with a wallet?"

Sighing in a weight-of-the-world manner, Jonathan dug into his pants pocket—fortunately his funds had not been in either back pocket, which had been burned away with the seat of trousers—and produced some colorful bills. Several of these he tossed in the window, got another scowl for his trouble, and the vehicle tore away.

"I don't mean to a stickler for detail," Jonathan said, with an eyebrow arched, "but how exactly does one—even if one happens to be a reanimated, two-thousand-year-old, terra-cotta Emperor—bring bronze horses to life?"

Glumly, Alex said, "He has mastery of the elements—earth, metal, wood, water and fire."

Frowning, O'Connell said, "That explains it."

Jonathan, both eyebrows up, said, "Oh, yes, that explains it quite nicely. After all, what a crashing bore a mummy would be without supernatural powers."

O'Connell, doing his best to be patient with his

130

brother-in-law, asked gently, "Jonathan, could we go inside? Some of us may have worked up a thirst."

"Well, you know it *is* after hours," Jonathan said archly, and then he fiddled in his other pants pocket for his keys and found them and went over and opened the door.

Evelyn, taking charge, gestured as she said, "Come on, everybody—inside!"

"Yes," Jonathan said, "please. Drinks are half price."

The proprietor of Imhotep's flipped on the lights and the room, with chairs on top of tables, looked somehow both bigger and smaller, empty of customers and employees, the mock-Egyptian decor exposed for the Hollywood-style sham it was. Jonathan ambled over and turned the lights on at the bar and got behind there to provide service. Shortly, every one was grouped loosely at and near the bar.

Evelyn had a hand on her son's shoulder. "Sweetheart—are you all right?"

Alex frowned at her, though he did not remove her hand. "If you two hadn't blown my position, I would have killed the bloody Emperor."

"We were only trying to help, dear." She drew her hand away. "To save you."

"Did I look like I needed saving?"

Actually he had, and did; he was perhaps the filthiest and most bedraggled of all of them, with the exception perhaps of Jonathan.

But she said, "No, dear, of *course* not . . ."

His chin crinkled, much as it had when he was ten or eleven. "You don't have to keep looking over your shoulder at me. I can hold my own."

O'Connell, having heard this exchange, said, "Didn't exactly look that way tonight."

Alex turned to his father, frustrated. "You should be *happy*—you've raised another mummy! Now you can play the big hero, just like in the good old days."

"I don't believe," O'Connell said evenly, "that I dug this one up, not in the first place, anyway. I believe that was . . . *you*."

Shaking his head, waving his hands, Alex said, "Don't try to pin this one on me! Er Shi Huangdi wasn't up and walking around when *I* found him!"

Evelyn got between them, a palm on either man's chest. "Stop it, you two! Nobody's to blame here. Alex, your father had no intention of robbing your glory much less play hero. Rick, you know as well as I do, that you and I and for that matter our son were all manipulated by Roger Wilson."

Neither father nor son could deny that.

Jonathan, wrapping some ice in a towel for O'Connell, said, "We could go back to the museum and you two could kick Roger's head around awhile. I'm sure even old Roger wouldn't object, at this point."

The dark comedy of that made both O'Connell men smile, if not at each other.

Jonathan handed his brother-in-law the ice-packed towel, and Alex moved down the bar to where Lin rested against it. Even with soot on her face and with her dark coat ripped to pieces from the knees down, she was an exotic vision.

Alex said to her, "I apologize for my parents."

"No need. They did what they thought was right."

"You know, Lin, we worked really well together tonight."

"We did. Except, of course, for one detail."

"What's that?"

"We failed."

That threw Alex for a slight loop, but he rebounded, saying, "Yeah, well, you *could* look at it that way. I'm more of a glass-half-full kinda guy myself."

Behind the bar, Jonathan, bringing his nephew a Coke and the young woman a glass of wine, said, "I'm more the who-the-bloody-hell's-been-drinking-out-of-my-glass sort of bloke, personally. And here's yours. . . ."

In the mirror behind the bar, Evelyn had been watching her son and the lovely Chinese girl speak. After Lin's eyes found hers, Evy came over and held a hand out to her.

"I'm sorry—we haven't been properly introduced. Who exactly *are* you?"

But Lin did not immediately answer. She waited until tempers had cooled and everyone, minimally cleaned off, had gathered at one large table, with drinks provided by their host.

With all eyes on her, Lin said, "For centuries my family has watched over the Emperor's tomb."

O'Connell exchanged glances with Evy—this struck a familiar chord: their friend Ardeth Bay and the fabled Med-jai warrior priests had similarly guarded the tomb of Imhotep at Hamanaptra, the City of the Dead, in the Sahara.

But that been told in Evy's novels, too, and Lin could be an impostor with a cover story essentially written by Evelyn O'Connell herself. . . .

Alex nodded toward the dagger in Lin's jeweled belt. "Where did the snazzy dragon dagger come from? That standard issue for tomb guardians?"

"Not exactly," she said coolly. "The weapon has been passed down through the generations of my family. The blade is enchanted, if I may use such a term among archaeologists and scholars."

Evy said, "You may."

O'Connell said, "I shot the ear off our clay buddy the Emperor *twice* tonight . . . and it regenerated in seconds. So we're pretty open-minded about this kind of stuff, Lin. Go ahead."

Lin smiled faintly and nodded. "Only *this* blade can kill the Emperor. But it must pierce the dark heart of Er Shi Huangdi to do so."

Evy was studying Lin with what O'Connell could read in his wife as suspicion, though that might not have registered on the others. She looked to him, and then to their son, and said, "Alex, darling? Might we have a quick, private family meeting?"

Alex shrugged. "Sure." He smiled at Lin and

touched her shoulder, then joined his parents, who had stepped away from the table and out of the young woman's earshot.

Whispering, Evy said, "What do you *really* know about this girl?"

Alex glanced back at Lin, then met his mother's eyes. "Admittedly . . . not much. She did attack me at the tomb. . . ."

O'Connell said, "Ah."

"But," Alex went on, "that's consistent with what she says about her family being guardians of that tomb over the generations. And after her help tonight, I'm willing to go on a little faith."

O'Connell and Evy exchanged unsure glances.

"I saw her try to kill that Emperor Mummy," Alex said, "tonight." He had also witnessed her getting shot twice and surviving it without a scratch, but this he did not bring up. "Come on, Mom, Dad . . . we've got a mummy out there with a good head start on us, and I don't believe either one of you is getting any younger."

Lin's voice, just behind them, came: "Time is running out."

They turned to find her standing right there.

O'Connell frowned and said, "You are *familiar* with the concept of privacy, right?"

She ignored the rhetorical question and got down to business: "The Emperor has the Eye of Shambhala— you may know it as the Eye of Shangri-la. If he reaches the place your culture knows as Shangri-la, and drinks from the Pool of Eternal Life, Er Shi Huangdi will become flesh and blood again, and raise his terra-cotta army . . . and all hope will be lost."

Jonathan had wandered over and now said, "Much as I might like to take a swig from the Fountain of Youth, and stay this boyishly handsome forever, isn't this Shangri-la a myth or, as we say in polite society, a load of bollocks?"

O'Connell shot him a look. "You used to feel the same way about reanimated mummies."

Jonathan shrugged. "Valid point."

Evy, her attitude different having heard Lin speak at more length, focused her attention on the young woman but spoke to them all: "The legends of the Eye mention a so-called Gateway, the location of which has always been shrouded in mystery."

Jonathan smirked in irritation. "Why must these legends always be so obtuse? Can't they just spell it out for once?"

Lin said, "The Gateway, like Shangri-la, is no myth. It is in the Himalayas. Once the Eye is placed in the crown of the stupa, it will point the way to Shangri-la."

"Now that's more like it," Jonathan said with a grin. "Straightforward and to the point . . . I like this girl. Uh, by the way, what's a 'stupa'?"

Evy said, "A domed Buddhist shrine . . . Lin, how do you know all this?"

"Yeah," Alex said, eyes on the young woman. "How?"

Lin gave him a blank look. "Perhaps saving your skin is not my only talent."

Then she beamed at him, and he grinned back at her. The romantic sparks between the young duo were not lost on Alex's mother.

O'Connell, however, was oblivious, perhaps because he was fixed upon other concerns. He asked Lin, "Can you lead us there?"

"I can."

Jonathan made a clicking noise in his cheek and smiled wide. "Alex, my boy, this one's a keeper."

Before Alex had time to be embarrassed, his mother asked Lin, "But you still haven't told us who you *really* are. Your family guarded the Emperor's tomb. Your name is Lin. What *else*?"

Lin's shrug was as gentle as her smile. "Let me help you, and you will find out more."

Evy thought about that, then shrugged herself. She glanced at her husband as if to say, *I can accept that.*

His nod said as much to her.

"All right," Evy said, and nodded crisply. "Now . . . obviously, we'll need to charter a plane, and at very short notice."

"Yes we will," O'Connell said. "And I believe I know just the right dog for this fight. . . ."

The best thing that could be said for Maddog Maguire's plane was that it was enclosed. This was not a relic of World War I, no biplane like O'Connell's late friend Winston Havlock had piloted, on a flight that had required Jonathan to be roped to one wing and Ardeth Bay to the other.

But it *was* a relic, and it rattled like one in the cross-currents. Maguire was of course at the controls, with only God as his copilot, and in the frayed, crowded seats to his rear, Evy and O'Connell sat side by side, with Lin and Alex close behind them, while Jonathan was stuffed in back, sharing the heavily piled luggage area with a drool-dripping, quite hairy yak.

Evy and O'Connell were turning shades of green that went nicely with their attire, she in a red heavy fur-trimmed coat with a bold green-and-white-striped sweater and green pants with high laced-up boots, he in a brown leather jacket with lighter brown fur trim/lining, and a dark woolen scarf knotted around his neck, also with high boots up his brown trousers.

Even Alex, in a black stocking cap and dark blue jacket with fur trim, seemed shaken by the ride, as did Lin in her brown jacket with fur trim and hood. Jonathan's brown jacket had more fur than anyone elses—not counting the yak, anyway.

And yet all that fur could not combat the cold the plane allowed in, and they all shivered, whether from the chill or fear or both, who could say?

From the cockpit, Maguire called back, "Any self-respecting pilot would land on the valley floor. Of course, I don't have any damn self-respect, so I'll set you down halfway up the mountain, instead."

Evy, through chattering teeth, said, "Thank you! That will give us a nice advantage. . . ."

"No extra charge, luv. 'Course, I can only guarantee you'll be halfway up the mountain. Can't guarantee you'll be *alive* at the time. . . ."

Evy glanced sharply at her husband, who said, "He's always been a card."

Maguire was saying, "Jonathan, you old reprobate! How are you *doing* back there?"

Jonathan was staring at the yak, who was staring back, drool dripping (the yak, not Jonathan).

"Peachy," Jonathan said. "Just tickety boo . . ."

At the training camp near the ruins of the ancient Ming village, the troops were lined up in formation as General Yang and the Emperor Mummy were chauffeured through in an open jeep. Er Shi Huangdi sat erect, his bearing imperial, exuding power. As the vehicle passed, the soldiers would break formation to prostrate themselves before their terra-cotta emperor, and when the jeep pulled up before the crumbling temple that was Yang's headquarters, the soldiers began to fire their weapons into the air and cheer wildly, madly.

The general escorted the Emperor into the command center, where, behind Yang's desk, the huge map of modern China was on the wall on display. Immediately, the Emperor Mummy strode to the map and began to study it, intrigued.

"Welcome to twentieth-century China, my lord,"

Yang said in ancient Mandarin, keeping a respectful distance.

The Emperor Mummy swung his head to turn the dead unblinking eyes on his servant. *"Why have you raised me?"*

Yang took two steps forward. *"The China of today is in chaos. I knew only our greatest emperor and his army of warriors could restore it to its rightful glory."*

The Emperor Mummy turned back to the map. *"And what do you hope to gain for yourself?"*

General Yang swallowed. His chin went up. *"I hope only to serve you as your faithful general."*

Again the lifeless eyes swung Yang's way. *"My last general was faithless. The last general betrayed me, and left me as you found me."*

Yang bowed his head. *"I would never make such a mistake. I live to serve you, my lord."*

The Emperor Mummy's dead gaze gave away nothing. Finally he said, *"I cannot raise my warriors—they are as statues, lifeless, as was I."*

Now Yang dared to approach. *"I understand, my lord—that is why I found the answer that you spent a lifetime seeking."*

The living statue tilted its head ever so slightly.

Yang went on: *"I have found the secret to eternal life."* And from a pouch at his hip, he withdrew the blossomed Eye, and held it up. *"This, the Eye of Shambhala, will point the way."*

The Emperor Mummy's chest filled and something strange appeared on his reddish-brown countenance: the faintest of smiles, and the most chilling.

The old gray plane, fitted with skis, dipped toward the towering, rugged Himalayas, the fabled "abode of snow." As the plane dove, the pilot worked his voice up above the propeller din.

"I'd tell you lot to fasten your seat belts," Maguire shouted, "but I was too damn cheap to buy any! So kiss your arses good-bye, and hang on tight!"

Then the pilot took a generous snort from a bottle of Jameson's—no passenger dared complain—and pushed the plane into a hair-raising decline. The aircraft swooped between two jagged outcroppings and dropped toward a narrow strip of snow. Soon the aircraft's skis, touching down, were kicking up a blizzard of snow and ice, and the plane began to bump and skid violently across the midmountain snowfield.

O'Connell had once heard the expression "All landings are controlled crash landings." This may not have been a crash landing, but it certainly seemed barely controlled, a ride almost as rough as that bronze steed had given him.

Maguire was cackling maniacally as he gripped his controls, and his passengers were hanging on to whatever they could—in Jonathan's case, the yak with one arm (his other hand held a paper airsickness bag).

141

"Come on, you little ripper!" Maguire commanded, his grin surprisingly white in the midst of all that dark stubble.

Then the plane went flailing, whipping in a circle that created more green faces and many white knuckles and a sea of popped eyes. Finally—finally—the crate spun to a stop.

"How's *that* for a smooth landing?" Maguire said, looking back at O'Connell with a cocky grin.

O'Connell grinned back—he had decided strangling Maguire was out of the question, since they would presumably need a ride home—and said, "Smooth as a three-day beard, Maddog."

Around him, O'Connell noted, everyone was ashen-faced; the green, at least, had faded. Something foul was in the air, though, and Evy's nose was twitching at it.

"What," she asked, "is that god-awful smell?"

All eyes turned to Jonathan, whose airsickness bag was overflowing. He gave them a don't-look-at-me expression, then nodded toward his hairy companion.

"The yak," he explained, "yakked."

Maguire up front said, "Welcome to Tibet, boys and girls."

·❮ 7 ❯·

Gateway to Paradise

The Himalayas

Pristine white peaks pierced the blue sky like shark's teeth, but Maddog Maguire, sitting on an apple box in the snow, was not terribly impressed. He'd seen mountains before, and in fact he'd even seen these. Warm in his well-weathered, fur-lined leather flight jacket, the stubbly-faced Irishman was hunkered near a field stove making himself a gentlemanly cup of tea.

What was on his mind was his own weakness as a negotiator—he had allowed his old Foreign Legion comrade, Ricochet Rick, to pay him in two installments—once for the flight to the mountains, and then another later for the flight back. Since the odds were against Rick and his little party ever returning, this had not been the shrewdest bargain Maguire had ever made.

His attention was drawn by a rumbling roar that he knew was a plane—C-119, he reckoned—but it was not coming from above him, no—rather, from the valley below. He got up from his seat and moved to the plateau's edge, where, from behind a boulder, he watched his suspicion confirmed as a C-119 glided in and touched down.

The Fairchild C-119 Flying Boxcar was a transport aircraft, perfect for conveying troops, which Maguire soon saw was the case here—a general followed by a bizarre martial figure of reddish brown were the first out, succeeded by several scores of troops in gray military winter uniforms.

Maguire thought, *There goes my second payment,* and headed for his radio.

Daylight was dying and they had to keep moving.

The trek up the mountain was not so steep as to be impossible but steep enough to make Alex O'Connell's legs ache, and he was a very fit young man. The snow had an icy cutting edge as it did its best to discourage them as they trod the path between the mountainside and the rocky shelf. Alex could not help but harbor some resentment, stuck back here toward the tail of their little procession. He would have rather been at Lin's side—she was up front, using a gnarled walking stick more suited to a crone than a young girl, but the way was rugged, after all. Meanwhile, he was stuck back here helping Jonathan encourage along the horned hairy beast piled with their supplies and armaments.

Even his mother was in front of him, and his father of course was right behind their girl guide.

"Listen, Jonathan," Alex said, his breath pluming, "can you handle this beast of burden?"

"Might I ask why your father has your lovely mother," Jonathan said, eyes hooded, face ice-flecked, "and you have the delicious Lin, whilst I have been paired with a yak? Just wondering . . ."

"Thanks, Uncle Jon," Alex said, and moved over snowy, rocky ground, past his mother and father, catching up with Lin.

"Hi," he said.

She glanced at him, but said nothing.

"You know, I read up on Tibet once, and it said monks stay warm by generating body heat. So, later, when it gets even colder, if you need someone to, well, rub up against you for warmth? I'm your man."

Her withering look cut him worse than the whipping snow.

She moved on ahead of him, using her stick as support, and the boy thought, *Smooth, Alex, real smooth . . .*

From the radio strapped to the yak came the voice of their pilot: *"This is Delta Tango Alpha to Ricochet. Come in, Ricochet."*

O'Connell, in sunglasses (even late in the day the glare of the sun off the snow could be blinding), fell back and yanked the mouthpiece from the two-way radio, walking along with the beast that bore it, Jonathan at the rear.

"Come in, Delta Tango Alpha."

"You know those two fellas you said should I should look out for? Well, I believe they just pulled into town with all their best boyos."

"Those fellas," of course, were General Yang and the Emperor.

O'Connell signed off, then moved back up in front of Evy, calling, "Okay, people! We've gotta pick up the pace—*move!*"

In the process of trying to do as O'Connell asked, Lin slipped, and Alex was right there to catch her, and help her regain her footing. He was unaware, as was Lin, that Alex's mother had noted the charged energy between them. . . .

By sunset, the little party had reached its destination for the night—the ruins of a monastery on a windswept hillside swathed in alpenglow, looking idyllic against a Maxfield Parrish sky of rouge and purple.

As they tramped toward this shelter, Evy—who had fallen in alongside her husband—said to him, "By my estimate, we have a half day's lead."

O'Connell nodded. "Still, we can't be sure. We'll

sleep in shifts and keep an eye out for Yang and the Emperor and their troops."

Walking backward, O'Connell called out to the rest of the party: "Packs on backs and feet to the ground at dawn!"

There were no arguments.

In what had been the main chamber of the ancient monastery, Evy stoked a charcoal campfire, surreptitiously watching her son and the Chinese girl as they unpacked supplies from the yak. To Evy, in the flickering half-light of the campfire, the couple seemed in full-on flirting mode, and the unpacking was taking forever.

Finally Alex crossed to his mother, a box piled with blankets in his arms.

Alex said, "According to Lin, if we leave at first light, we should reach the Gateway by noon."

Evy nodded. "Did she happen to say how she knows so much about this Gateway?"

"Not really." Alex glanced back at Lin, and when his face returned to his mother, his features were touched with a goofy lovesickness that did not encourage Evy as to his objectivity. "She's kind of . . . mysterious. Enigmatic."

"Well," Evy said, with a smile as icy as the weather, "she's certainly managed to enchant *you*."

Alex frowned at his mother in confusion. "What do you mean?"

She rolled her eyes. "Oh, Alex, what I mean is, you've spent the entire journey thus far trying to impress this girl. You are *obviously* attracted to her. Nothing wrong with that."

Alex smirked, shook his head. "I think this mountain air is clouding your mind, Mother."

Evy tilted her head and her eyes sent her son a signal of concern. "Whatever secret she's hiding, son, I want you to take care. I don't want to see you get hurt."

Alex did not react defensively. He said, "I appreciate that, but . . ." And then he assumed an unearned air of self-confidence in the ways of women. ". . . I mean, it's not like I haven't had my fair share of *experience* with the opposite sex."

His mother did her best not to betray her amusement. "I guess a mother doesn't really know when her little boy has grown up. How many . . . 'experiences' . . . are we talking about? One, five, ten . . . ?"

He lifted his chin and blustered along: "You shouldn't ask questions when you don't want to hear the answer, Mother."

"I see. I see. Well, I appreciate you protecting my gentle sensibilities." She studied his face, trying to look past his bluffing. "Experience is one thing, Alex, but tell me this—have you ever been in love?"

And now the line had been crossed: Alex was clearly uncomfortable continuing this particular conversation with his mother. Still, he could not help but contemplate the subject she'd raised, and his eyes drifted to Lin, still dealing with the supplies.

"I haven't been in love yet," Alex admitted, surprisingly frank. "At least, not like you and Dad . . . Look, I gotta go. Lin and I have first watch."

"Stay alert."

"Will do." He started to go, but stopped and turned back to his mother. "Listen—I'm sorry about being such a brat . . . you know, blaming you and Dad for raising the Emperor from the dead and all."

Evy was quite sure this particular apology had never been made to a mother by a son before.

"That's quite all right, Alex," she said. "This specific mummy has managed one feat I didn't think possible, no matter how many elements he's the master of."

"What's that, Mom?"

She gave him her warmest smile. "He's brought the three of us together again."

Alex's smile in return was immediate and natural and the very same smile he'd been giving his mother since he was a very small child. She had seen it a thousand times, and treasured every one.

He strode off, and Rick came over to her wearing a wary expression.

Craning to look back at his son, he asked Evy, "What was that about?"

"We were just catching up," she said lightly.

Rick nodded. "How's he doing?"

149

"Fairly well, I think. You might go over there and talk to him yourself, and find out. . . ."

He glanced over, but Lin and Alex were stacking supplies, laughing together in what was obviously a private moment.

The boy's father said, "I think he's a little preoccupied."

Evy's mouth twitched in a tiny smile. "He claims he's not interested in her. Or anyway, not in love with her."

"I should hope not." Then her husband's brow furrowed and he said, "Of course, you made the same claim about me, when we first met. You said you despised me."

She shrugged. "Fine line between love and hate and, anyway, those were entirely different circumstances."

He walked her behind a half wall, finding a little privacy, looking at her in the old way; he stroked her cheek, gently, very gently. "As I recall, we were stuck in the middle of nowhere with a rampaging mummy on the loose. Seems like similar circumstances to me. Déjà vu all over again?"

She smiled, and touched his face. "Who knows what will happen after we get to that Gateway tomorrow?"

"You're right," he said, and edged closer.

She swallowed and continued, "Mummies being such an unpredictable lot . . ."

"Hmm-hmm. But so are the O'Connells."

Their lips were centimeters apart.

"Still," she said softly, "one never knows. . . ."

"Knows what?"

"When one . . . when *we* . . . might be spending our last night together."

"Well, then . . . we better make it memorable."

And their lips met, the kiss as deep as it had been in the desert when they first triumphed over Imhotep, as passionate as in the hot-air ship over Ahm Shere after their second adventure. They, and their love, were suddenly young again—reanimated without any magical elixir.

Snow battered the half-crumbled edifice, washed in blue-gold moonlight. Seated near the campfire within the mostly roofless structure, Jonathan Carnahan spoke with a companion.

"We all of us have a burden to carry in life," he said philosophically, "but nobody's denying that yours is a considerable one. May I call you Geraldine? . . . That was the name of a schoolgirl I once loved, and somehow I think it suits you. I mean, I can't go around just calling you '*yak*,' now can I?"

The beast was resting nearby, providing almost as much warmth as the fire.

Jonathan continued: "After all, you're so much more than just a 'yak'—in fact, we're all very proud of what you've accomplished."

A sort of grunting emanated from within the big hairy body.

"Yes, my girl," he went on, rhapsodizing, "if only I could find a woman with your fine qualities—loyal, hardworking, not prone to prattle on." He glanced at Geraldine. "I would prefer less hair, but no one can deny you have lovely eyes."

A nightmarish howl seemed to rend the night itself beyond the crumbling monastery walls—*what the hell kind of creature was* that*?* he wondered.

The wail echoed in the darkness, like a cry from beyond the grave, and Jonathan, shaken, slipped an arm around Geraldine's neck and clung to her.

"Is it all right," he asked her, "if I hold you for a while? I'm sure you'll find it comforting. . . ."

Geraldine had no apparent objection.

In the adjoining chamber, blankets around their shoulders, Alex and Lin had just gotten to their feet. They'd been enjoying the glow of the fire that burned in the center of the foundation, giving nicely dim illumination to every partial-walled room.

And then Alex had heard the ungodly howl that had so startled Jonathan, and stood, and so did Lin, although she claimed not to have noticed the ghastly cry.

Then another roar echoed beyond the half-fallen edifice.

Alex's eyes were wide as he turned toward the sound. "There it is again! You must have heard it *that* time. . . ."

She shrugged. "It's nothing. Probably just a snow leopard. They are more afraid of us than we are of them."

Alex thought, *I'm not so sure,* but then changed the subject, standing facing her. "You know something funny? My mother is under the impression that there's something going on between us."

Her expression turned incredulous. "Not something *romantic*? How foolish of her."

Alex was a little hurt by this, but he didn't show it, as he said, "I told her there was no chance of that."

"Right. Good."

"I mean, look at us—we're complete opposites. You guard tombs, I raid them—what kind of basis for a relationship is that? I like guns, you're into knives. These are pretty insurmountable odds, after all."

"Absolutely."

My God, she was lovely in the glow of that fire, her face going in and out of darkness as the flames flickered. . . .

Alex half grinned and said, "Good. Fine. Now that we have that cleared up, we can stay focused. Keep our eyes on the prize."

"The prize?"

"Taking down the Emperor."

"Ah. Yes. I could not agree more."

Silence draped the small room. Shadows from the fire wavered over them. Then he looked right at her.

"I mean, hell," he said. "You're not even my type."

"That's obvious," she said. "Why would you want a woman who can knock you on your backside?"

"The current expression is *kick your ass*, and just for the record, you didn't."

He'd barely finished that when she threw a wicked right cross at him, which Alex caught, like a firefly he'd grabbed out of the air.

Then he drew her close to him. His face approached hers; her face approached his. The sexual charge between them was something neither could resist, although Lin tried.

She said, "This is a bad idea."

"Terrible. The worst."

So he kissed her. And she kissed him back, and there had not been a kiss this passionate, this epic, in a very long time . . .

. . . not since Alex's father and mother kissed, a few minutes before.

The snow stopped falling but the wind kept blowing it around, so the next morning's ascent was similarly rugged, Lin and O'Connell leading the party single file up the narrow, snow-covered path, which snaked around the near-vertical face of a gorge.

Finally, Lin gestured and said, quietly, "There . . ."

O'Connell saw it, too, and called back excitedly, "We've *found* it!"

They had indeed found the Gateway of Shambhala,

154

or as the awestruck Evy spoke aloud, "The Gateway of Shangri-la."

A monumental colonnade of stone forged the gap between two mountains, accessible by an ice-encrusted rope suspension bridge.

Within minutes, they were headed across, where on the other side, on the steps and among the columns of the Gateway, O'Connell began to lead his little group in preparation for the ambush of an ancient Chinese Emperor with a contemporary paramilitary force.

Jonathan was excused from these preparations to attend to the yak, feeding her handfuls of shredded wheat biscuits. "Don't you worry about me, Geraldine— better men have tried to kill your companion than some sorry old red-clay, Chinese mummy. You just stay safe and, if anything should perchance happen to me, you go find yourself a nice young yak to settle down with."

Geraldine grunted and licked him with a tongue as disgusting as the gesture was affectionate.

In the rocks near the Gateway, O'Connell dropped his weapons trunk and proudly cracked it open, revealing an impressive portable arsenal of revolvers, assorted automatics, a pump twelve-gauge, a Thompson submachine gun and more. He turned to see Alex approach, a trunk of his own over a shoulder.

"Okay, son," O'Connell said. "The toy box is open—help yourself and tool up . . . just be sure to save a few goodies for your old man."

Alex half smiled. "Hey, thanks, Dad—but I excavate relics, not use 'em to shoot with. Besides, I have my own box of toys."

O'Connell's son cracked open his trunk to display an array of gleaming revolvers and automatics with a shotgun and submachine gun thrown in for good measure, all looking as shiny new as cars on a showroom floor.

"What did you do," O'Connell said, impressed, "rob an armory?"

"Actually," Alex admitted, "I won 'em in a high-stakes poker game."

He frowned at the boy. "Since when did you start playing high-stakes poker?"

"Since boarding school with my allowance. Think back—that's what I got kicked out for the *second* time . . . remember?"

O'Connell frowned. "All those schools and all those infractions kind of blur together after a while."

Alex selected a glistening snub-nosed pistol from his trunk. "You ever use a Walther P-38, Dad?"

"No. Looks like a peashooter compared to the Peacekeeper."

O'Connell withdrew from his trunk a long-barreled blue .45 revolver worthy of Wyatt Earp.

Alex seemed only amused. "Dad, don't you know? It isn't about size—it's about stamina."

"Is that right?"

The boy nodded. "Your gun's spent after six rounds. Mine just keeps pumping."

O'Connell, finding this conversation vaguely disturbing, reached in and grabbed a tommy gun. "You want power, son, I defy you to beat the Thompson submachine gun. One hundred rounds a clip."

"Yeah, right. That baby's swell . . . if it's 1929 and you're chasing Al Capone. Don't you find that it always jams? I mean, *always*?"

O'Connell's brow furrowed. "Does not."

Rather than get into a "does so" debate, Alex said, "Here, check out this Russian PPS-43 Personal Assault Weapon. This is the future, right here."

O'Connell did not take his son up on the offer, saying, "It's experience that saves the day, Alex, not firepower."

"You learn that back in the twenties, too? Anyway, you were just singing the *Thompson's* praises."

The father and son had reached a point of uncomfortable stalemate.

Jonathan came ambling over. "Boys," he said, "if I may—have we developed a plan of any sort?"

O'Connell said to both of them, "The Emperor may have mastery over metal and what-have-you, but he's not immortal yet. We're going to hit him hard and hit him fast, and smash his ass like a Ming vase."

Alex had a skeptical expression. "Didn't we more or less try that already?"

"Yeah," his father said, "but we didn't have enough firepower."

The argument had come full circle, but Alex didn't say so.

Jonathan said, "Bloody brilliant—firepower. Good show. But, huh, Rick—if firepower should happen *not* to work . . . ?"

O'Connell said, "That's where Plan B comes into play, Jonathan—you're going to blow the bastard sky-high, if he makes it upstairs to that little temple."

"Excellent plan, that should . . . *What? Who?*"

"You."

Jonathan's eyebrows climbed to his hairline. "I am? Really? Me?"

"That's swell, Dad," Alex said skeptically, "just so long as the explosion doesn't kill *us*, too. Of course, if we survive, the *avalanche* can always get us."

O'Connell scowled at his son. "You have a better Plan B, I suppose?"

Alex nodded. "I say we ambush the Emperor with long-range rifles with silencers. Before they know what hit 'em, we'll get in close and finish old clay boy off with Lin's dagger."

Shaking his head, O'Connell said, "Alex, I'm not putting my faith in your girlfriend's magic knife."

"She's not my girlfriend . . . but that knife *is* magic."

O'Connell waved his hands like an umpire calling a runner out. "I don't trust her."

Alex gestured to himself with a thumb. "Well, *I*

do. So I think you should trust my judgment, for a change."

The father knew dangerous ground was being trod on here.

Carefully he said, "Look, son, it's not a question of whether I trust your judgment or not. It's just that I've put down a few more mummies in my time than you have. We'll do this *my* way."

Alex held up a forefinger. "You've put down *one* mummy, Dad."

"One mummy *twice* . . . and all his minion mummies, too."

Alex shut the lid on his gun trunk. "Well, if it were me, ol' Imhotep and his minions would have stayed down for good, the *first* time around."

From among the nearby stacked supplies, Alex grabbed a box stenciled DYNAMITE and began to climb toward the courtyard where the small domed temple called a stupa awaited.

O'Connell shook his head and said to Jonathan, "I swear, if that kid weren't my own, I'd shoot him myself."

Jonathan, his face framed in the fur of his parka, said, "Congratulations, old boy—you have a son who is independent, questions authority and approaches life without trepidation. Sound like anyone you know?"

Scowling again, O'Connell said, "Yeah, well, it's *still* damned annoying."

With that, O'Connell trudged off to make more

preparations, leaving Jonathan alone, looking across the precarious suspension bridge.

"Well, Geraldine," Jonathan said. "At least I have you."

But he didn't—the yak had gone off and left him truly alone with his responsibility as the man in charge of Plan B.

·❨ 8 ❩·

Abominable Conditions

B eyond the suspension bridge, the ancient stone front columns of the colonnade, topped with the images of long-forgotten Tibetan gods, provided an elaborate entryway to the snow-covered courtyard, stalactites of ice hanging off every undercarriage. At the center of the courtyard was the small temple called a stupa, a single-story dome with a graduated, stairstep-style outer shell with four squared-off stone entryways and crowned in a golden spire that caught the afternoon sun in glinting glory.

That such a historical treasure might be destroyed saddened Evelyn O'Connell, but the stakes today were much higher than that. With luck, her husband's Plan B would not have to be set in motion. But for now, archaeologist Evy O'Connell was helping the enigmatic Lin finish wiring the charge, the stupa now crisscrossed with sticks of dynamite.

Kneeling, Evy said to Lin, "Hand me the red wire . . . no, make that the *blue* one."

Lin's almond eyes appraised Evy critically. "Are you sure you know what you're doing?"

"Of course," Evy said with cool confidence that she did not feel. "I've done this kind of thing a hundred times. Two hundred . . . It's definitely the *red* wire."

Evy clipped the wires into place, then turned to Lin. "I know you have your share of secrets, young lady . . . but Alex is naive in the ways of the heart. Promise me you won't hurt him."

Rather solemnly, Lin said, "I promise."

The two women, Evy in her red fur-trimmed coat, Lin in her brown hooded one, tramped back to the columns of the colonnade.

Evy said to the girl, "Good—because otherwise I'd have to kill you."

Lin glanced at the woman, to see if this was a joke.

But that remained ambiguous, though Evy was now smirking and saying, "Of course, we'll probably all die today anyway, so perhaps the point is moot."

And the two females Alex O'Connell cared most about in the world exchanged tentative smiles that became a sort of truce before a battle with other, shared foes.

* * *

Rick and Alex O'Connell crouched behind columns, scoping out the terrain. To their rear, up the steps, higher columns above provided firing positions for Evy, Lin and Jonathan, ready with weapons trained.

Last night, O'Connell had thought his wife had never looked more beautiful; seeing her with a Winchester in her hands, with a smile anticipating this adventure as much as he was, he decided she was at her loveliest, today.

Earlier Jonathan had inquired why they hadn't wired the bridge to explode as well, but O'Connell explained that, first, they wanted to lure the Emperor Mummy to his doom; and second, the O'Connell party might like to leave here, themselves, at some point. . . .

"Ah," Jonathan had said. "And without the suspension bridge, that might prove difficult."

"Bingo."

O'Connell, spotting some movement, nudged his son, and nodded toward the bridge and the rocks beyond; from around the bend emerged a line of rifle barrels. He grinned at Alex, said, "Let's give them a warm O'Connell welcome," and Alex grinned back and nodded.

O'Connell and Alex opened fire, and then so did Evy, Lin and Jonathan. The thin Himalayan air cracked and snapped with gunshots and went thick with lead and gun smoke as Yang's heavily armed, helmeted troops in full winter gear poured into view, streaming across the bridge single file, firing as they came, slugs carving out chunks of stone from the ancient columns, blasting away ancient faces that would be now and forever lost to history.

After picking off the first two soldiers, sending them over the side of the bridge, screaming their death throes as they fell, O'Connell kept at it, and so did Alex, and they exchanged tight smiles, feeling good about how Plan A was going so far—these poor bastards were sitting ducks.

Behind the enemy lines, Er Shi Huangdi was not impressed either with twentieth-century warfare or his new general. Irritated, the terra-cotta Emperor said in ancient Mandarin, *"You send them to their deaths! Change your tactics."*

Yang nodded and deployed two men with bazookas, keeping them on his side of the suspension bridge, and ordered, *"Fire!"*

Two bazooka-fired rockets streaked across the chasm and the resulting explosions seemed to shake the world, several columns disintegrating, the entire facade of the colonnade crumbling down.

O'Connell and his son had pitched themselves out of harm's way when the rockets came toward them, but they'd been within seconds of being crushed under falling chunks of stone and showering rubble.

To the trio in the next row of columns, O'Connell called, "Pull back! Pull *back*!"

And Evy, Lin and Jonathan, with O'Connell and

Alex right behind, moved deeper into the courtyard, to reconnoiter.

Behind enemy lines, Er Shi Huangdi demanded of Yang, *"Who* are *these people?"*

Yang, expressionless but sweating despite the cold, said, *"They are but a minor irritation."*

A couple of bullets pocked the Emperor's brown clay chest, to him less than a gnat bite; automatically, the bloodless wounds sealed. *"Clear a path to the stupa. Show me you are as good a general as you claim to be."*

Yang's chin went up; he bristled at the challenge, but accepted it unhesitatingly. From his pouch he removed the blossoming gem that was the Eye of Shambhala. He handed it to the Emperor, with a curt bow, saying, *"Immortality is at hand, my lord."*

Beyond the columns, the O'Connell party was taking the steps up to the stupa, two at a time, Alex looking back to fire, twice, with a rifle, knocking out the bazookas in a most effective way: hitting the weapons themselves, exploding them to uselessness as well as taking out four soldiers, who went tumbling into the abyss, shrieking in pain that would soon be over.

But this victory proved minor, since the rest of Yang's forces were now racing onto the bridge.

O'Connell and company were gathered, with not much cover at all, at the base of the small steps leading up to the one-story stupa.

"Jonathan," O'Connell said, "I would say it's time for Plan B."

Nervous as hell, Jonathan said, "I was wondering if we might try Plan C instead."

"What Plan C?"

"I was hoping *you* had one, up your sleeve. . . ."

O'Connell's eyes and nostrils flared and he got in his brother-in-law's face. "We have to blow that dome to Kingdom Come! You're on deck, Jonathan—we'll cover you."

"Fine, and if the explosion gets me, bits and pieces of *me* will soon cover *you*. . . ."

Jonathan stayed behind, at the stupa's base, as the others moved along the periphery of the snow-covered courtyard, often with massive icicles above them like crystalline swords of Damocles; they stopped at the crumbling brick walls at the rear, to take cover.

In the meantime, Yang and his men were charging up the steps toward the courtyard, maintaining perfect rifle-company formation, leapfrogging and covering their exposed positions.

At the base of the dynamite-wired golden stupa, Jonathan had dropped to his knees, and was getting out his trusty Dunhill lighter. But when he tried to get the bloody thing to light, it was no go—not the Dunhill's fault, Jonathan knew, rather his own trembling hands.

First to appear in the courtyard was Yang, shouting orders in Mandarin. O'Connell, from behind a side column, fired off a few quick shots at the general, whose attention was drawn that way, and with a handgun Yang returned O'Connell's fire. At the same time, troops hustled around the general's flanks and set up their own positions, firing and diving behind columns and steps.

Finally, Jonathan got a flame going, and was about to light the fuse when shots chewed up the snow inches from him, and he instinctively pitched the lighter and scurried for cover, muttering, "Damnit to bloody hell! That was a gold-plated Dunhill!"

Then Jonathan cut a zigzag path back to O'Connell and Evy, who were together now behind a half-crumbled brick wall.

Elsewhere, Alex was dashing behind a partial brick wall himself as shots pocked around him. He withdrew a roll of electrical tape from his pouch and began to bundle three sticks of dynamite into a makeshift bomb.

At the same time, Alex's uncle had dived behind that broken wall while Evy provided cover, pumping away with her Winchester, winging a soldier who'd been getting too close, and winning a glance of admiration from her husband.

A startled Alex saw Lin break from cover and run toward the rear of the colonnade, where stood a torii-style gateway. Though she was for the moment at the far side of the fray, Lin was nonetheless out in the open and making a perfect target, much to Alex's dismay. She seemed to be staring up at the open mountain slope behind the colonnade; *had she lost her mind?*

"Lin!" Alex yelled, and went scrambling after her.

Yang's brutal onslaught just went on and on, the general and a few helmeted soldiers advancing to the stupa while others inched their way up the courtyard on either side, ducking the bullets of Rick and Evy O'Connell, who exchanged desperate glances as they reloaded.

O'Connell said to his wife, "I guess we've been in worse scrapes."

Evy said to her husband, "Really? If we survive, you'll have to remind me. . . ."

Then a haunting howl cut through even the gunfire, that same mournful bellow that had been heard in the darkness the night before.

O'Connell and Evy's eyes went to the rear of the colonnade, where, centered within the torii, stood the source of that strange sound—*Lin herself!*—her hand to her face as she delivered the ululation, like Tarzan calling for the animals of the jungle to come to his aid.

Bullets puffing the snow chased Alex as he ran to the torii within which Lin stood, eyes on the mountainside and the surrounding hills, and half a second after he tackled her, rolling with her to relative safety, strafing gunfire chewed up where she'd been.

That gunfire was still pounding away when a howl like the one Lin had somehow summoned from within her lithe form came down from the slope, horrific and otherworldly, a sound that could stand the hair up on the back of a human neck.

Three shaggy forms came charging down from the hills—at first they seemed to be big men in long fur coats, but quickly they became something else: creatures, nine feet tall, covered in gray-white fur, with smallish heads for such large and powerful frames, with mouths opened wide to show off fierce fangs.

Yang's men stared in disbelief but so, for that matter, did Jonathan Carnahan, behind the half wall of bricks with his brother-in-law and his sister. "My God, can those bloody things be—"

"Abominable snowmen?" O'Connell said, between submachine-gun bursts. "Yeah."

"Actually," Evy said, between Winchester rounds, "the Tibetans prefer 'yeti.'"

"How quaint." Jonathan threw his sister a withering glance, fired several shots at Yang's men from his own rifle, then said, "Well, by all means, let's defer to *them* on the subject. . . ."

Neither husband nor wife seemed particularly surprised about such bizarre reinforcements showing up, but perhaps, Jonathan thought, that was because they were preoccupied with the forces of a reanimated mummy.

And the Yeti indeed seemed to be reinforcements, as Lin dashed out to them and shouted something guttural in a tongue unknown to Jonathan or for that matter O'Connell and, for all her expertise with antiquity, even Evy herself. The creatures were roaring something in response that seemed half animal cry, half spoken word, and then raced by her, apparently doing her bidding.

O'Connell turned to Evy. "Well, now we know a little more about our son's girl—she apparently speaks yeti!"

Evy said, "Fluently, I should say . . ."

A yeti jumped from the roof of a side building and down into the courtyard, sending up flurries of snow with his feet. The other two yetis were already on the attack, charging toward the forward-flank soldiers, who—as Yang commanded, *"Shoot! Kill them!"*—raised their carbines to take aim, but not in time. The yeti were upon them to bat away the weapons and grab the soldiers and effortlessly fling them into a nearby stone wall, where the helmeted men thudded and crumpled, like flung rag dolls.

Panic quickly spread among Yang's men, and the O'Connells took full advantage, father and son charging from either side of the colonnade, with Evy and Lin right behind, attacking a force of far greater numbers but dealing with shocked, distracted, terrified troops, who fell like carnival-midway targets.

The only hitch was when O'Connell's Thompson jammed, earning him a quick I-told-you-so smirk from his son, whose Russian assault weapon was still doing just fine.

Thinking, *I hate it when the kid's right,* O'Connell found himself staring down an enemy's rifle barrel. But one thing that never jammed was Rick O'Connell's hand-to-hand combat skills, and he snatched the weapon away from the man and used it to beat him senseless.

O'Connell wheeled to find another soldier bearing down on him with a big knife, held high; grabbing the man's wrist and giving it a vicious twist, O'Connell broke the bastard's wrist and then knocked him cold with a good old-fashioned right hook that dumped him on the snowy courtyard floor.

Lin and Evy were also showing off their hand-to-hand skills, more than holding their own with several clearly well-trained martial-arts experts among Yang's men, one of whom was unlucky enough to be on the receiving end of an Evelyn O'Connell spin kick, which deposited him in the arms of a yeti, who promptly flung him like a javelin into a brick wall.

Yang's men, however panicked, were managing to hit the trio of yeti now and then, but the slugs seemed to do little more than mildly ruffle the creatures' fur. The general himself fell back into the small stupa, unaware Alex had ducked in to change ammo, and walked into the boy's fist.

Blocking the punch, Yang threw a high kick and knocked Alex to the floor of the little structure, then shoved his right boot heel into the young man's larynx, pinning him painfully.

"Your adventure, young O'Connell," Yang said through a small, rare smile, "ends *now*. . . ."

But before Yang could deliver a deathblow, a hairy arm reached into the small temple and grabbed the general, yanking him across the interior of the stupa, and through its front entryway, and flung Yang with a momentum that sent the general unceremoniously tumbling down the short flight of steps, bouncing right past the Emperor, who was moving into to the courtyard. Without a glance at, or a thought for, his injured general, Er Shi Huangdi stepped over Yang and moved calmly on through the chaos of battle.

Of all the remarkable feats of bravery on either side—though clearly such feats were more the domain of the O'Connell party—one stood out that afternoon: Jonathan Carnahan, on his hands and knees, crawled through the melee of gunfire and hand-to-hand combat and yetis committing carnage to find his way to his lost Dunhill lighter. Recovering it, Jonathan crawled on to return to the dynamite-strung stupa and, cackling with self-worth, he finally lit the fuse.

"Yes!" he said. "Piece of cake . . ."

Still staying low, Jonathan then turned to crawl away and almost bumped into two huge gray-white legs. He smiled up at a yeti, who looked down at him curiously, the way a monkey might regard a baby bird with a broken wing.

"I say," Jonathan said cheerily, getting cautiously

to his feet. "Wonderful, brisk weather we're having, don't you think? Enough snow for you?"

The yeti roared in Jonathan's face—*what* had *the thing been eating?*—and Jonathan, his moment of bravery past, went running pell-mell toward the walls near the rear of the courtyard.

But as Jonathan ran, something strange occurred—even for a day that already included a terra-cotta Emperor Mummy and a trio of yeti—as a great cracking filled the air, like an ice floe breaking itself into pieces. Huge stalagmites of ice burst from the snowy stone floor of the courtyard, massive yet with points as sharp as the tip of a stiletto.

All of them were in danger—O'Connell, Alex, Evy and Lin and Jonathan, too—and had to run a serpentine course to keep from being impaled. The yeti bounded up on the roofs of the side temple buildings, showing themselves capable of caution and good sense.

Only from the entrance to the courtyard to the golden temple of the stupa, with its stairstep walls leading to the gleaming spire, did a clear path remain.

And down this path walked the rust-brown figure of Er Shi Huangdi, who—spotting Jonathan's fuse—waved a hand and dispatched a knife blade of ice to cut the fuse in half, causing it to fizzle out.

Seeing this from behind half a brick wall, Jonathan muttered, "Definitely not cricket . . . these damned mummies just don't play fair. . . ."

Into the now-empty courtyard strode the Emperor

Mummy, head up, exuding arrogance like heat over asphalt. As he walked, nearby icicles retreated into the snowy courtyard floor.

O'Connell ran up the cleared path and threw himself onto the stupa wall, and began scaling the stairsteplike side. He would beat the son of a bitch to that spire, where if Er Shi Huangdi applied the Eye, all was lost. Alex threw down fire to cover his dad, and even caught the Emperor Mummy with a good volley, for all the good it did.

Almost to the top, O'Connell could see clearly the spire that was the prize, glinting in the sun. What he could not see, on the other side of the stupa, was the smiling Er Shi Huangdi simply touching the little temple and turning O'Connell's steplike path into a sheet of ice, down which the adventurer slid fast and landed hard against an icy stalagmite.

O'Connell was in the Emperor's view now and Er Shi Huangdi extended a hand and an arm, the red clay heating up, glowing white-hot; his fingers made a tiny gesture that produced a big fireball that shot out like a meteor at O'Connell, who scrambled out of its path even as it exploded and toasted his heels.

Behind the cover of a column, Alex was readying his homemade bomb. . . .

The Emperor had climbed the stairlike side of the stupa and was placing the blossomed Eye in the depression atop the temple golden spire. The Eye began to glow and a rodlike beam of icy blue light shot out, careening against a series of ancient mica reflectors, and finally pinpointing a declivity at the mountaintop opposite.

On a tiled roof nearby, Lin watched, and waited. . . .

On her cue, Alex charged out into the open and, as Lin had told him to do, threw the bomb not at the Emperor, but up the mountainside, to disrupt the transformation Er Shi Huangdi intended to initiate.

But the Emperor Mummy could see what Alex was up to and a sword materialized in his terra-cotta hand, and he hurled the blade, sending it pinwheeling toward Alex's back.

O'Connell dove in and pushed his son out of the way, but caught the sword himself, as it cut through his back rib cage and pushed all the way through like a skewer.

Alex's bomb exploded short of its target, the blast sending thundering reverberations throughout the hills and mountains nearby. But the boy's eyes were elsewhere: his father had collapsed facedown in the snow. And the Emperor Mummy's sword had returned by magic to his red-clay hand, then retracted into nothing at all.

From behind her half-a-brick wall, Evy watched, white as the snow around her, moaning, "Oh, God . . . dear God . . ."

Alex's scream of sorrow met the echo of the blast and the mountainside reacted, a cornice of icy snow letting loose high up, signaling what was to come. . . .

Jonathan, not helping matters, screamed, *"Avalanche!"*

And indeed the shelf of snow and ice was beginning its deadly journey their way, creating an earthquakelike rumbling that froze even the yeti with fear.

Alex ran to recover his father, or anyway his father's body, and dragged him toward the entry.

The Emperor, still up on top of the stupa dome, saw shelf after shelf of snow and ice come rushing toward him, and knew even his powers would be tested here. His mouth opened and he emitted a furious roar as he raised his arms, throwing all of his mystic power at the mountainside.

Gradually, starting at its base, the avalanche began to slow, more and more snow massing in piles, but those massive white mounds seemed to be struggling against the invisible force that sought to keep the avalanche back, natural and supernatural locked in a savage struggle.

Lin had edged along the roof and, dragon dagger in hand, was closer now to the distracted Emperor; when she was opposite him, she leaped, dagger raised, but Er Shi Huangdi turned, as if he'd heard the buzzing of a mosquito, and with a glance deflected her—she was flung to a pillar and slid down into a semiconscious pile.

The living statue that was Er Shi Huangdi returned all of his attention to the tidal wave of snow and ice, concentrating every particle of his fury at it. But after the Emperor Mummy's momentary distraction, the wall of snow was again speeding unfettered toward the courtyard. . . .

Near the entry, a yeti swooped up Alex and the wounded O'Connell and bore them away, toward a portico. Jonathan, unfortunately, was petrified in horror, like a Pompeii victim, watching the avalanche inexorably heading his way. Deeper into the courtyard, Evy was helping the dazed Lin to her feet, the girl seemingly unaware of the white wall descending. Then another yeti swept in, and hauled them both away in its powerful arms.

Jonathan couldn't seem to make his feet and legs work. He spoke what he felt sure would be his final words. "Bloody hell!"

But his cry was lost in two mingled roars: that of the white tidal wave slamming into the temple, and the shriek of a yeti.

The terra-cotta mummy received the full brunt of nature's blow, getting knocked off the stupa and pistoned right through the columns, getting buffeted from one pillar to another like a pinball between bumpers and finally shattering into a thousand rust-brown shards that were quickly lost in a merciless sea of white.

Another player was attempting to outrun the avalanche, though he was in no shape to be doing so: limping along came a very bedraggled General Yang, looking like he'd already been put through as many indignities as humanly possible.

But he hadn't, because a shelf of snow now slammed him down the front staircase and all the way onto the suspension bridge, as the courtyard seemed to spew snow at the beleaguered general. Torqued by cascading white, the bridge snapped and sent Yang tumbling toward the abyss.

Within minutes, the snow was still again, and the world settled, and quiet reigned. The landscape had a peaceful look, as if nature had held sway here for centuries and no man had set foot since ancient times.

The courtyard was piled with snow and crisscrossed with fallen trees. Finally a yeti burst from a bank to sniff the air. He took several steps, knee-deep in the stuff, which was many feet in some areas and only inches in others, and, after continuing to sniff for a scent, punched into another bank, fished around, and yanked out Jonathan Carnahan, like a gopher the creature had snagged, holding him one-handed by the leg.

"Well done, you ugly brute," Jonathan (dangling upside down) said with genuine gratitude. "A Saint Bernard could not have done better, although it's true such a beast would no doubt have come equipped with a little barrel of brandy. Wouldn't happen to have one of those on you, would you?"

With a dismissive snarl, the yeti dropped Jonathan, as if he were too scrawny a catch to keep. Then the great creature pulled Evy up and out, followed by doing the same for Lin, lifting each out of the snowfield.

On their feet again, the two women, unsteady at first, found purchase between drifts, but Evy was clearly alarmed.

"Rick!" she called. *"Rick!"*

The muffled voice that replied belonged not to her husband but her son: "Over here, Mom! Over here!"

A yeti thrust himself upward out of the snow and revealed an air pocket, where Alex cradled his father. "Come on, Dad! *Say* something. . . ."

Very weakly, O'Connell replied, "Guess we've been . . . in tougher scrapes . . . than this. . . ."

Then his eyes rolled back in his head as what little consciousness he'd had left him.

A desperate Evy, at his side, put her cheek to his. "*Stay* with us, darling . . . stay with us. . . ."

"There is only one way," Lin said.

All eyes, even the yetis', went to the slender girl.

She said, "We must take him to Shangri-la."

·❨ 9 ❩·

A Dragon in Shangri-la

The crevasse at the Gateway to Shangri-la was filled with snow and was now as quiet, as lifeless, as a landscape painting. Peacefulness had settled over an area where recently men with weapons had fought, and a great battle for the soul of the world itself had been waged. Now all that seemed over. A crisis for mankind, with only a few of its number knowing, had been averted.

Then, as if to give lie to such an assumption, vertical recessions along the top of the snow-packed crevasse began to form, indicating something burrowing underneath, small animals creating berms, perhaps. One after another, the recessions formed and all seemed to angle toward a central spot, like a spider-web. Had anyone had been above, on the edge of the crevasse, to look down and to witness it, this might have seemed some natural if bizarre phenomenon.

But it was not.

The fragments of the terra-cotta mummy, each possessed of dark life, were seeking one another and now, to join in a blast of heat at the center of so much cold, re-formed themselves into a recognizably human, if still terra-cotta, shape.

The Emperor Mummy rose as if on an elevator up through the surface of the packed snow, and silently surveyed the scene. His eyes fell upon the pitiful if resilient and most certainly battered form of General Yang, holding on to what was left of the suspension bridge, its remnants disappearing into the snow-choked chasm.

The miraculous reassembly of the shards of Yang's terra-cotta master had been largely without sound, just whispers of movement in the snow below, and the general had after all been preoccupied just trying to stay alive.

But when the Emperor called out—*"General!"*— Yang looked down fifty feet to where, defying all odds, his master stood atop the snowfield, and—ever the zealot—the dangling general nodded and called, *"My lord!"*

"Come! Our destiny awaits!"

Yang nodded dutifully, and awaited more specific instructions, which came in the form of a gesture from the Emperor, creating from the snow a stairway of ice so that Yang could join his master, who had already turned to create a second stairway leading up into the snow-ruined Gateway to Shangri-la.

Alex O'Connell felt like hell. Never in his short life had he been so guilt-ridden; he had treated his father so terribly in recent days, and now the elder O'Connell was on the brink of death, after sacrificing himself for his son.

In this vast Himalayan world, the members of the O'Connell party—expanded to the improbable tune of three yeti—were just so many specks moving along a passage carved in a sheer cliff. They were on their way to Shangri-la, if Lin was to be believed . . . and of course Alex believed her.

Even had they wanted to go the way they'd come, that suspension bridge was history now; and the slender girl who could communicate with yeti had assured them that safe passage to Shambhala (as she often called it) was possible, and from there an alternate route back would be available, as well.

And if Alex wanted his father to survive, Lin had told him in no uncertain terms, a visit to Shangri-la would be Rick O'Connell's only chance to face adventure another day.

The hooded Lin and Jonathan—yakless now—were leading the way. Up ahead was another gorge with its own small, rather unreliable-looking wooden bridge. Two yeti were carrying the unconscious

O'Connell on a stretcher Lin had made with the help of these creatures, using pine boughs interwoven with fragments of Tibetan prayer flags. Evy walked alongside her husband, holding his lifeless hand. Alex was on the other side, his gut knotted with guilt.

"Faster!" Alex urged, his voice reverberating through the nearby gorge. "We need to go *faster!*"

"I say, nephew," Jonathan said gently, "another avalanche wouldn't help any of our situations."

When they crossed the precarious bridge over a seemingly bottomless drop, the little party did so fearlessly—even Jonathan. They'd seen enough, and survived enough, to take peril rather more casually.

Past the bridge, still on the narrow carved-out path, ever upward they went, until finally Lin spied an outcropping of rocks. "We're here!"

The outcropping marked the small mouth of a cave, and through that mouth and into that cave was where Lin led them. But none of the O'Connell party, even after all they had witnessed on this and other expeditions, could have been prepared for what they saw.

Though the passage into the cave was cramped, it quickly opened into a vast cathedral of a cavern. Along the left wall, with its head toward them as they entered, was a slumbering statue of Buddha no larger than the *Queen Mary*. On the other walls were carved-out native statues and dwellings like those of cliff-dwelling Indians back in America.

But for all this, what stood at the center of the natural chamber was the most impressive. Haloed in sunlight pouring in from the far side of the cave, which had at one time collapsed to reveal the out-of-doors, was an open pavilion in the Tibetan style, with pillars and a stupa-style roof, a storybook structure surrounding and protecting the serene blue of a pool, shimmering incongruously in the midst of this amphitheater of rock, refracting rainbows of light.

Evy thought, *The Pool of Eternal Life!* Her husband might yet survive. . . .

Her son echoed this, pointing and shouting, "The pool!"

The yeti lowered the stretcher to the rocky floor as an excited Alex dashed into the cavern, making a beeline for the pavilion. In a blur, a figure in flashing green came streaking from above and landed in front of him, drawing a sword from a back sheath.

Alex froze and saw before him a striking if cold-eyed woman, a streak of white in the otherwise ponytailed-back dark hair—in her thirties perhaps, but blessed with a timeless beauty.

Alex's estimate of the woman's age was off somewhat: he had no way to recognize her, or to realize just how timeless her beauty was; but the woman in the green flowing robes with the sword in hand ready to dispatch him was Zi Yuan, the sorceress who had, two thousand years before, cursed Er Shi Huangdi—to his terra-cotta doom.

Before he could react, Alex found Lin at his side, and the younger woman was meeting that sword blade with the edge of the dragon dagger, making a metallic clunk that echoed in the yawning chamber.

The woman looked sharply at Lin, who with her free hand dropped her fur-lined hood to give this guardian of the pavilion a better look at the one who'd dared interrupt her defense.

Then Lin dropped to her knees, in supplication, and touched the woman's slippers tenderly. Zi Yuan stared down in utter shock, then gently raised the girl up, tears in both their eyes.

In an ancient strain of Mandarin, Zi Yuan said, *"Lin, my little love."*

"Mother."

And the two women embraced. They had not seen each other in some time—in fact, in many centuries.

The yeti, accompanied by Evy, were bringing up Alex's father on the stretcher to where Zi Yuan could see their human cargo, who was groaning, as if death were moments if not minutes away.

Evy stepped forward and said, quietly, "Would you please help him?"

In English, Zi Yuan said, "You are friends of my daughter, and you are welcome here."

Alex and his mother exchanged startled glances, but Evy had the presence of mind to say, "We are very grateful. What may we call you?"

"Zi Yuan."

The yeti deposited O'Connell on his stretcher near the edge of the pool within the simple interior of the pavilion. Zi Yuan herself administered the Elixir, cupping it in one hand from the blue pool and gently pouring it onto O'Connell's bloody wound.

Li Yuan asked, "Who harmed this man?"

Evy, nearby, said, "This man is my husband, Rick O'Connell. Some might not believe it, but I have a notion you will have no problem when I say that that wound came from a sword wielded by an ancient Chinese Emperor, who now walks the earth as a terracotta monster."

The woman's eyes flashed. "Er Shi Huangdi," she said.

Evy, Alex and Jonathan all exchanged glances.

Then Zi Yuan rose and said, "Your loved one is out of danger now."

Evy knelt and kissed her husband's forehead, then gazed up at Zi Yuan with happy, tearful eyes. "How can I thank you?"

The woman bowed slightly. "You already have."

Off to one side, Alex and Lin stood together and he was staring at her, considering this "young" girl in a whole new light.

He said, "Then . . . Shangri-la is your home?"

"Yes."

Jonathan, close enough to hear without trying, thought, *And here I thought the girl talking to yeti was a bit odd. . . .*

187

To Evy, Zi Yuan said, "Your husband must rest now."

She indicated her own dwelling nearby, carved out of the rock, and led Alex, Lin and Evy, bearing the stretcher, to a stone stairway up into it. Jonathan had been having a look at the pavilion, walking around the exterior of it, touristlike, and stumbled onto a view of the far section where the cave wall had long ago given way to reveal a vista beyond.

He gaped in awe. "Bloody hell . . . It's paradise."

The cold snowy world from which the O'Connell party had come was nowhere to be seen—this was a perfect spring day under a nearly cloudless blue sky, a heaven on earth ringed with endless silken waterfalls, a breathtaking landscape of flowers and greenery and sunshine.

When Jonathan turned around to tell everybody about this Elysium, he saw they had trooped up stairs carved out of the cavern into a similarly carved-out dwelling space. He followed and was soon at his sister's side, tending to O'Connell.

Minutes later, Alex, Zi Yuan and Lin strode back down the stairs to speak.

Lin's mother's face was taut with urgency. She said to her daughter, "Did the dragon dagger pierce the Emperor's heart?"

Lin shook her head. "No, Mother. I have failed you."

But Zi Yuan stroked her daughter's cheek and gazed upon her with compassion. "I should never have let my vengeance become your burden . . . but you were not to involve mortals in these affairs."

Lin gestured toward the dwelling, and nodded toward Alex. "If not for their bravery, the Emperor would have found the pool."

"And yet he still may, now that he has risen."

Alex jumped in with a grin. "Excuse me, ma'am, but don't worry about ol' clayface. He's at the bottom of a gorge in a million terra-cotta pieces."

Zi Yuan shook her head. "If he was not killed by the dragon dagger, then he is not dead."

Alex frowned. "How can you be so sure?"

Her chin raised; light winked off golden earrings. "Because I am the one who cursed him. I enchanted his own dagger and dispatched the only person who could be trusted to watch over his crypt while I stood sentry over this sacred pool."

Frowning in curiosity, Alex asked, "If I'm not out of line . . . ? What did the Emperor do to make you hate him so much? To make him worthy of such a curse?"

Her face was placid and so was her tone, but in Zi Yuan's eyes, fires of vengeance burned. "He murdered the only man I ever loved—Lin's father. For that I cursed him . . . and his army, as well."

Zi Yuan held out her hand and Lin gave her the dragon dagger. She stared at its blade, her bitterness reflecting back at her.

"I would have died, too," Zi Yuan said, "at the

monster's hands . . . and yes, he was a monster even before I cursed him . . . but the yeti found me, and brought me to this pool."

Though math had never been his strong suit, Alex knew something was adding up strange. He turned to Lin and asked, "So, uh . . . how long exactly were you guarding the Emperor's tomb?"

Calmly, without expression, as matter-of-fact as answering a phone, Lin said, "Two thousand years."

Alex drew in a breath. His eyes widened. He let out the breath.

Lin steeled herself.

Zi Yuan had more important concerns. She was moving into the cathedral of rock, heading back toward the entrance through which the O'Connell party had come.

"The Emperor must not reach the pool," she was saying, "or he will have the power to raise his entire army. . . . You two stand guard here, at the pool itself. I will take first watch at the entrance."

Elsewhere as the sun began to set and wash the rugged snowscape in scarlet light, the Emperor Mummy and his general climbed. . . .

For what seemed like a long time, and which was perhaps two minutes, Alex and Lin sat on the steps of the pavilion, guarding the pool in awkward silence.

Finally Alex said, "For the record, you don't look a day over one thousand. . . . It's a joke. You look incredible, period."

That made her smile. "You are very sweet, Alex."

"Again, for the record? I just want you to know—I have nothing against dating an older woman."

But she shook her head. "I am afraid we cannot be together."

He blinked at her. "Why?"

"Because I am going to live forever, and you aren't. You will grow old and you will die. And I care for you too much to watch."

He thought about that. Then he said, "So, instead of giving the two of us a chance at maybe having something great, you're just going to sit on the sidelines . . . for all eternity."

She avoided his eyes. "My mother has mourned my father for many centuries. I do not know if my heart could bear such a burden."

He leaned in, not wanting to let her off the hook. "You know what *I* think, Lin? I think, immortal or not, a man and woman in love can live an entire lifetime . . . in just one look."

She cocked her head and finally met his eyes. "How can you say such a thing?"

"Because I've seen it. I watch my parents do that every day."

From above, from a window in the carved-out dwelling, Jonathan called, "Alex! Your father's come around!"

He was up like a shot, and took the short flight of stairs the same way.

191

Zi Yuan's chambers were decorated with almost monastic simplicity, and yet also bore a feminine touch, in splashes of colored fabric. On the simple, palletlike bed, O'Connell awoke to find Evy on one side and Jonathan on the other.

Looking at his wife, O'Connell said, his voice husky but surprisingly strong, "If this is heaven, it's looking good so far."

She stroked his head, then tangled her fingers in his hair. "If you ever leave me like that again, Rick O'Connell, I'll kill you myself."

Then, at the same time, they decided to kiss each other and did so in a passionate way usually reserved for either the end of the adventure or at least until they were alone behind closed doors.

From the entryway, Alex's voice came: "Nice to see some things never change."

O'Connell noticed something tentative in his son's tone, despite the jaunty words.

Evy leaned close and whispered, "Go easy with him, darling. He blames himself for what happened to you."

O'Connell got to his feet—without much trouble, surprisingly—and his son crossed to him.

Alex said, "When I saw you on the ground, all bloody like that . . . I was never so scared in my life."

O'Connell grinned. "Well, that makes two of us."

The boy shook his head, his eyes moist. "You're not supposed to die, Dad—you're Rick O'Connell,

Ricochet Rick, remember? They can beat you up, toss you around, but you'll still be standing at the end. I can't really picture this world without you in it."

The father, pleased but embarrassed, shrugged. "Son, I'm just a regular guy, trying to be a good husband and a good father. But as a husband and father, I guess sometimes I make a good mummy hunter."

Alex laughed; so did his dad.

"Son, lately I've been dropping the ball. I'm sorry."

The boy twitched a half smile. "Well . . . I haven't exactly been in line for a World's Greatest Kid trophy myself."

O'Connell shrugged again. "You must get that streak from your mother's side."

Father and son hugged; then the boy's mother joined them. It was a sloppy, sentimental moment and it was wonderful.

Taking a few moments away from standing watch at the cave entrance, Zi Yuan—the dragon dagger tightly in her grasp—slipped back into the cavern to speak privately to her daughter, who sat within the pavilion, staring at her own reflection in the pool. Then her mother's reflection appeared there next to hers.

Lin turned to the woman, who sat beside her and touched her hand, gently. In ancient Mandarin, Zi Yuan said, *"You look tired. You should rest."*

"I will stay here and keep watch. We both have our responsibilities."

The mother squeezed her daughter's hand. *"I am sorry you have spent your life paying for my sins. For centuries I have dreamed of the moment when you would return to me."*

Lin swallowed. *"So many times, Mother, I have wanted to come home . . . knowing that I could not."*

Zi Yuan nodded. *"And now fate is about to deal its final hand. And if we are to defeat the Emperor, I must ask you to make one more sacrifice."*

"Anything, Mother."

"You must give up your immortality."

Lin frowned in confusion.

"Let me explain. . . ."

But before Zi Yuan could do that, a comet of fire streaked across the cavern from behind them, a tongue of flame that seemed to lick the dragon dagger right out of Zi Yuan's grasp and at the same time knocked both women onto the pavilion floor.

Striding into the cathedral-like cave with Yang trailing just behind, the terra-cotta mummy extended a hand and drew the dagger back to his own grasp, then returned the blade to a sheath it had left many, many centuries before. The dead eyes flashed with surprising life upon seeing Zi Yuan.

In the cave dwelling above, summoned by disturbing sounds, the O'Connells ran to a window carved from the stone and looked out onto the pavilion and pool. O'Connell, Evy, Alex and Jonathan all watched in horror as the Emperor Mummy strode up the short steps into the pavilion and waded into the blue waters, sinking deep, the red-brown clay figure disappearing beneath its surface.

All four ran from Zi Yuan's chamber down the steps into the cavern and seemed to hit the brakes simultaneously as before their wide eyes the pool began to course with energy, swirling with ominous force.

"My God," Evy said. "All of his powers will be fully restored . . . *forever*. . . ."

Then, slowly but inexorably, the Emperor's head began to rise above the blue, swirling surface; *but terra-cotta no more!* This was Er Shi Huangdi's human face, breaking the surface, only . . . then it happened again . . . an identical face bobbed up . . . and again . . . *three* Er Shi Huangdi faces!

"Third time," O'Connell said, his hand feeling for a sidearm holster that was no longer there, "definitely not a charm . . ."

Each head revealed itself to be attached to a long, scaly neck, and then as the creature rose farther from the water, the three long necks could be seen to extend from a thick, snakelike body. The Emperor had shape-shifted into the very three-headed dragon that had always been his symbol.

But there was nothing symbolic about the way the creature rose until it finally popped the canopy from the pavilion as if the wood and gold roof were papier-mâché, crashing it down onto the cave floor. Columns toppled, as the dragon moved menacingly across Zi Yuan's cave.

"Next time," Jonathan said, "if no one objects, I may stay home. . . ."

Proving it was indeed a dragon, the creature reared back all three heads and let loose torrents of fire, driving his enemies to cover. O'Connell had to pull Zi Yuan out of the way, as streaming fire scorched the cave around them, and Jonathan led Evy behind the slumbering Buddha, for cover. General Yang, running alongside the dragon, jumped into its taloned grip. Lin was against a wall, where she'd been flung, and was coming around just in time to see six mustard-colored eyes glow at her with vengeful lust.

From a charred recess where he'd taken cover, Alex jumped out and screamed, "Get *away* from her!"

But the dragon grabbed Lin in its left taloned foot and batted the boy away with a folded wing. And as the dragon swept past, Alex made desperate eye contact with Lin, promising her silently he would save her somehow, even though right now he was helpless to.

Then the creature was gone, flying through and out of the cave. They did not see the thing, wings spread, filling the air, but the snapping sound of those wings they most certainly heard, as it flew straight up and out of their world.

The walls of the cavern were smoking as everyone reemerged from their respective cover. The smell of it was sulfurous.

With stiff dignity, Zi Yuan said, "Er Shi Huangdi is taking my daughter back to his tomb. He will raise his army."

Evy said, "Zi Yuan, is there a fast way down from here?"

"With the yetis' help, there is."

Alex was shaking his head. "But that thing is flying overland—we'll be too late."

O'Connell smiled grimly. "My bet is Maddog Maguire can outfly a three-headed lizard any day."

Alex looked more frightened than O'Connell had seen him look since childhood.

The father slipped an arm around his son's shoulder and squeezed supportively. "We'll get her back, Alex. We'll get her back, and make that monster pay."

·☾ 10 ☽·

No Regrets

The gray crate that was Maddog Maguire's plane was dwarfed by massive clouds in the nighttime sky. Not only had Maddog been game to fly his little party to the valley in Ningxia Province, China, where Alex had first uncovered the tomb of Er Shi Huangdi, the pilot seemed so relieved to see them alive—and able to pay him the balance of what was owed him—he might well have flown them to the moon and back.

From the extra space available in the otherwise cramped cabin, now that Jonathan's friend Geraldine the yak had moved on with her life, the party was able to—one or two at a time—make certain preparations for the warmer climate, including making changes of clothes. Only Zi Yuan had dressed for the trip before leaving her cavern dwelling—she was now in a flowing olive skirt, gold silk blouse and purple brocade vest, all subdued colors but for a splash of purple sash, attire she described as "battle ready."

The rest of the O'Connell party had left some of their baggage and clothing aboard the plane, in anticipation of another possible leg to the journey. Jonathan merely abandoned his heavy parka and announced himself ready ("if not entirely willing and able"), while Evy had gotten into a full-skirted brown dress over which she now wore a brown leather jacket with matching gloves, looking elegantly prepared for adventure.

Rick O'Connell, like Zi Yuan, was prepping for battle—light brown chinos, a blue-gray long-sleeve shirt (rolled halfway up the forearms) and a brown vest-style shoulder sling for his twin .45 revolvers. Alex, also in a long-sleeve shirt and chinos, had a brown leather coat on and both men were gloved.

The father had already opened up his weathered case of weaponry, filled with its mishmash of handguns, shotguns, an M3 submachine gun (the ever-popular "grease gun") and of course his prize tommy gun, which had jammed on him back at the colonnade. Alex was getting into a suitcase that brimmed with showroom-worthy Russian PPS 43s, the submachine gun Alex had sworn by and used so effectively in the recent struggle with General Yang's mercenary soldiers.

"You mind," O'Connell asked his son, "if I try out a couple of those?"

Alex glanced at his dad, and both men grinned—a divide had been crossed. They had finally bonded, even if it had been over submachine guns.

Their pilot called back to them over his engine roar: "Look, three-o'clock port! The boys back home'll never believe this yarn!"

O'Connell and Alex made it to the nearest port-side window and could see, thousands of feet below, catching the oranges and reds of dawn, the three-headed creature that Er Shi Huangdi had become, flapping its huge wings, heading east. Barely visible in a back claw of the beast was its unwilling passenger, Lin.

Alex stared at his love, far below, and fading. His father gripped his shoulders and squeezed. The two exchanged glances but no words were said. None were necessary.

Maguire's plane banked away, making a quick exit after delivering O'Connell, Evy, Alex and Zi Yuan to a designated drop point in the desolate valley, not far from the site the younger O'Connell had worked, seeking Er Shi Huangdi's tomb. Jonathan stayed on board with Maguire, as per plans O'Connell had put in motion. In fact, it was already time to check in with Jonathan.

O'Connell knelt and clicked on his shortwave. "Any sign of our flying friend?"

Jonathan's voice came back over the radio: "Negative. You better get a move on, though, if you're going to beat him to that tomb."

"Just do what I told you to," O'Connell reminded his brother-in-law, and clicked off.

The little party began to walk, four abreast. The morning was cool, but compared to the Himalayas, seemed damned near subtropical.

Alex, at his father's side, said, "Dad, I know we're good—no question otherwise. But the Emperor will have thousands of warriors, once he wakes 'em up."

But it was Zi Yuan who answered: "His terra-cotta army will not be indestructible."

Evy said, "Well, that's comforting."

Zi Yuan continued: "That is, not until they have crossed the Great Wall."

Frowning, Evy asked, "Meaning no disrespect, might I ask how exactly the four of us are going to fend these 'thousands of warriors' off?"

"When the emperor built the Great Wall," the serene sorceress said, "he buried his enemies underneath, cursing their souls to hold it up for him, for all eternity."

Alex said, "Tough boss."

Evy was ahead of her son, if not her husband. She asked the woman, "You know how to raise them from the dead, don't you?"

202

Expressionless, Zi Yuan said, "There is a Foundation Chamber with an altar dedicated to the five elements."

O'Connell said, "The elements Er Shi Huangdi controls."

"Yes. From this chamber, with those powers, the Emperor enslaved those souls, locking them in, so to speak. Most were captured soldiers who were then turned into slave workers. I will *un*lock them, using that same altar. And I will call them to battle, one last time. . . ."

O'Connell was nodding. "Unlock that altar, raise an army. Sounds like a plan."

His wife glanced at him. "An army of the dead," she reminded him.

"Right. Zombies. But *good-guy* zombies . . . on *our* side. That's the kind of living dead I can get behind."

Alex, walking along, was thinking how casually his father was taking all this. Of course, no one on earth had dealt with as many reanimated dead people as his old man, so he guessed he could understand it.

But Alex had not been at this long enough to be nonchalant, and until the two-thousand-year-old young woman he loved was freed from these literally evil clutches, he was unlikely to be.

The wasteland where Alex O'Connell had unearthed the Emperor Mummy once again had tents near the base of the half-exposed Sphinx-like monument Er Shi Huangdi had built in honor of himself twenty centuries before. This time, however, an archaeological expedition had been replaced by the gray-uniformed soldiers of General Yang. For days these men had been training and awaiting orders, hoping to hear from the general, and from the arisen Emperor who would lead them to victory.

They did not expect to hear from Er Shi Huangdi in the manner he chose, however, specifically laying a huge blue shadow over the camp and bringing all eyes to the sky, where a giant three-headed dragon went sweeping by.

With surprising grace for such an ungainly if grotesquely magnificent creature, the dragon dropped Yang and Lin to the ground before the colossus, right in front of the gathered soldiers, who numbered nearly two hundred.

Yang straightened himself, brushed off his uniform, and—mustering as much dignity as possible for a man just dropped from a dragon's claw—he summoned a cadre of soldiers and turned Lin over to them, saying in Mandarin, *"Guard her with your life."*

The dragon itself touched down beside the head of the colossus, like a parrot on a pirate's shoulder. The great beast folded its wings around itself, halving its size, then the necks with the three heads wrapped themselves around the trunk of the creature, melding

204

and condensing. The conversion was bizarre and freakish but the result was amazing.

There, standing next to his own commanding colossus, was Er Shi Huangdi, regal in his black, jade-encrusted armor, with his golden-hilted sword at his side and the dragon dagger sheathed at his waist. A vision of imperial power, he merely had to look at the assembled soldiers for them to immediately bow, awestruck.

General Yang, bowing his head as well, wore an expression rarely seen on this somber, serious, self-important man—a smiling one; but a smile touched with hysteria and greed. Though his eyes were on the scrubby ground, he was gazing into what he felt sure would be his future.

At the Emperor's right hand, Yang would himself live like an Emperor, guiding Er Shi Huangdi in the ways of the twentieth century. And he, like the Emperor, would live forever in the pages of history, and perhaps his lord would grant him the gift of eternal life, for without Yang, Er Shi Huangdi would still be but a bronze statue encasing a terra-cotta mummy.

Then, as was their wont, the soldiers began to cheer and fire their weapons in the air, celebrating the return of the general and, especially, their emperor.

Crouched low in a ditch, Rick O'Connell watched the celebratory scene through binoculars, thinking, *That's fine, boys—just keeping using up that ammo. . . .*

Next to him in the ditch were Evy and Zi Yuan, with Alex behind them, flat on his belly against a mound, using his own binoculars to see for himself.

O'Connell, after watching the situation at the colossus camp awhile, said, "Okay, Alex . . . you wait here with the shortwave, in case Jonathan and Maddog call. . . ."

Alex said nothing.

His father lowered the binoculars and turned to look; Evy and Zi Yuan craned to look, as well.

But Alex was nowhere to be seen.

Evy, alarmed, said, "Where did that boy *go*?"

His father, however, was not alarmed; he was even smiling a little, as he again raised the binoculars to see his son scurrying across the plain, keeping low, heading toward Yang's encampment. "Where do you think, my love? He's gone to save the damsel."

Then he led his little commando team, now reduced to two females (albeit remarkable ones), and they made their way toward the Great Wall, half a mile away.

Colonel Choi, missing in action since the Emperor's escape by chariot from the Shanghai Museum, was once again at General Yang's side. With him, she watched with keen interest as the Emperor, still up there on his own giant shoulder, withdrew his wide-bladed sword from its golden sheath.

Facing the empty landscape beyond the camp of

206

Yang's mercenaries, the Emperor plunged his blade into the stone, as easily as if the colossus were made of human flesh.

In a commanding voice, he shouted, *"Awake!"*

That single word echoed across the plain like ungodly thunder.

And the earth began to tremble, to quake, but not to break apart at its seams, rather to collapse in a dozen places, angling down as if providing ramps into—and up out of—the underworld. A drumming rumbled from the earth, not martial music, but feet, and not human feet, but hard-baked clay, as from each ramplike hole emerged terra-cotta soldiers, moving quickly, with murderous purpose, charging up and out of the hell of their long state of suspended animation and into the light of day, and onto the field of battle.

Rick O'Connell needed no binoculars to see the swarming soldiers now. He and the two women had made it to the Great Wall.

"My God," O'Connell said to his wife. "There must be ten *thousand* of them. . . ."

"If they get past the Wall, we don't stand a chance. The *world* doesn't stand a chance."

"Don't worry—Zi Yuan will give us all a chance, if . . . where *is* she?"

They turned and the sorceress, like Alex before her, was nowhere to be seen. She, too, had a job to do, her own job, and the O'Connells did not figure in.

"Us mere mortals," he said, "must not get to see the supersecret entrance to the Foundation Chamber."

"I'll forgive her," Evy said, an automatic pistol in either delicate, gloved hand, "if she raises those zombie reinforcements before that terra-cotta army catches up with us. . . ."

O'Connell knew better than to argue with his wife.

In the camp of yurt tents, one tent in particular had two guards positioned outside. They had been given strict orders that their lives depended upon guarding the young woman within. And yet they were human—seeing an army of terra-cotta soldiers march up and out of the ground had gotten their attention.

They didn't notice one of their number, or anyway someone wearing one of their gray uniforms, walking by with his head down. Had they not been distracted, Alex might have looked suspicious to them. As it was, the first they knew anything was when an unfamiliar voice said in Mandarin, *"Sweet dreams,"* and, one by one, the men got a rifle butt jackhammered into the back of their skulls.

The guards fell, still alive, though unlikely to be for long, after their general learned they had allowed their charge to be rescued.

Because that was exactly what Alex was doing—he went into the tent, untying the wide-eyed Lin, who said, "How can you be here?"

"A dragon didn't bring me," he said with a grin, "but you should've known I wouldn't give you up without a fight."

Her mouth frowned but her eyes smiled. "Oh, Alex. This is a bad idea. . . ."

"Oh, yeah. The worst."

Then he kissed her, and she kissed him, and the world stopped for a thirty-second eternity, as if the reality beyond the tent was not a reanimated Emperor Mummy, a megalomaniacal general, two hundred mercenary soldiers and a thousand or two terra-cotta warriors raised from the dead.

A massive stone door rolled back and Zi Yuan stepped into the Foundation Chamber, breathing in air that bore the staleness of centuries. She moved past the astrolabe and the waterwheel and down the walkway to the great stone staircase. On the domed ceiling high above were corpses protruding in macabre bas-relief, a portion of the souls enslaved by Er Shi Huangdi to hold up his Great Wall.

The sorceress climbed the many steps to the altar with its stations representing the five elements. Once there, from her garment she withdrew the Oracle Bones she had discovered in the library at the Monastery of Turfan on the Silk Road, so very long ago.

These bones she tossed in the air with a grace and

sureness of purpose, and they landed, unfolding for her to read from them, which she did.

In ancient Sanskrit she intoned the text: *"Open the gates of the past and free the souls of the wrongfully damned. . . ."*

On the rolling plain above, a sea of terra-cotta warriors had taken the field in lines—infantry, banner carriers, pikemen, archers, and cavalry, terra-cotta horses as well as soldiers. They marched with an efficiency that was a fascist's dream, until they came to attention before the Emperor, high above them on the shoulder of the colossus, saying in ancient Mandarin, *"Look to me and hear my purpose! Today you awake to a world in the grip of chaos and corruption. With your allegiance, I will restore order and crush the scourge that is freedom."*

And below, before the altar in the Foundation Chamber, Zi Yuan was saying, *"Open the currents of justice and the lost wave of honor. Bring down the wrath of the oppressed onto this evil Emperor and all who follow him."*

The dusty air began to stir.

Up above, the Emperor continued: *"I will slaughter without mercy. I will conquer without compassion. . . ."*

And below, Zi Yuan continued: *"In the name of the ancestors and the virtuous, in the body of the suffering, in the might of the one true cause, I sacrifice my immortality and that of my daughter so that you may rise this day and do righteous battle."*

On the domed ceiling, a skull shook itself loose, as one waking from a long, deep slumber; and then a bony foot extended itself, stretching. As she looked up at this gradual transformation in its beginning, Zi Yuan felt a sudden weariness, and though she did not see it, white now streaked her hair and gentle spiderwebs of age had formed on her face, as her immortality spiraled into the ether.

And above the Emperor was saying, *"I have raised you for one purpose and one purpose only—to enforce my will on the entire world! Only then will there be true peace, under my iron hand."*

The sound of cheering warriors—both human and terra-cotta—bled down into the Foundation Chamber, but another human sound, a moaning of awakening, could be heard when that martial roar died down.

Speaking from her heart, Zi Yuan said, *"I call upon the hundreds and the thousands to rise up and seize this moment, to take your victory, to take your justice . . . and to take your righteous revenge!"*

Over her head, a skeletal hand emerged from the bas-relief to shake itself with rage.

The Emperor was about to mount the black steed that was his warhorse when he felt the ground shift beneath his feet and the animal's hooves. Something

211

was in the air, as well. He frowned, sensing a shift in the very cosmos itself.

Then he said, quietly, for no ears but his own, *"Zi Yuan . . ."*

At the base of the Great Wall, Rick and Evy O'Connell waited, a Russian submachine gun in his hands, a pair of automatics in hers. They could hear and see the terra-cotta soldiers, heading their way. To say they were outnumbered was beyond understatement.

And then a trench opened in the dirt like a zipper along the base of the Wall.

O'Connell grinned at his wife. "Here come the good guys. . . ."

The good guys, the reanimated Foundation Army, burst out by the thousands, and never had a sight so horrific been such a relief to human eyes. These were figures in various stages of decay, with only scraps of apparel, yet full of sinew and stringy muscle, and alive with the iron-willed rage of the wrongly killed. With hardly a weapon among them, they nonetheless swooped onto the plain, ready to fight.

"A pretty motley crew, our side," Evy noted.

"I never saw anything so beautiful," her husband replied.

The two most unlikely armies ever to take the battlefield now moved into formation. The terra-cotta lines of the Emperor clanked into position, spears and shields up. The only representatives of the living were General Yang's forces, anchoring the red-clay warriors, at the right, left and center flanks with sixty or so men per, ready to teach the ancient soldiers all about twentieth-century armaments, or at least being on the wrong end of same.

General Yang, with the tall, lovely if scarred Colonel Choi at his side, positioned himself by his jeep, on which was mounted a .39-caliber machine gun. And the Emperor himself, no longer a mummy, sword held high, strutted on his high-stepping black stallion.

"Archers!" Er Shi Huangdi called to his terracotta men in the ancient version of Mandarin they knew so well. *"Form up!"*

The front ranks on each flank knelt, long bows in hand.

And through the front line of the assembled Foundation Army pushed a figure Zi Yuan would have recognized, despite his desiccated condition: another general, a long-dead general returned to make his last stand—Lin's father, Ming Guo. However the worse for wear *he* might be, Ming Guo's sword still gleamed in the sun.

O'Connell and Evy, from the sidelines, moved in quickly to approach this commanding figure.

"Sir!" O'Connell said. "We're on Zi Yuan's side of this thing."

"Uh, Rick," Evy said gently, "sweetheart—I doubt he speaks English."

213

Even so, the mention of Zi Yuan had registered on the time-ruined face.

The Emperor's voice echoed across the wasteland: *"Fire!"*

And a thousand arrows took flight as if toward the sun, but arcing down in a deadly swarm, a shadow of death stalking the battlefield.

O'Connell grabbed his wife by the arm, one of Alex's Russian submachine guns in his right fist, as they bolted toward a ruined foundation along the wall, its lintel broken. They dove underneath in turn, Evy first, as the deadly rain of arrows fell. They had little room to spare, two arrows pinning O'Connell's shirtsleeve to the ground.

The arrows had ripped into Ming Guo's line, as well, plunging through eye sockets and between ribs and sometimes shattering bones but usually doing not much harm at all. Ming Guo himself took a bullet that would have been in his heart if that organ hadn't long since decomposed; he plucked it out and threw it aside with a peal of ghoulish laughter.

Even Er Shi Huangdi could not kill what was already dead.

Their general's laughter spread through the ranks, a wave of defiance washing across the field as the skeletal soldiers wrenched arrows from their decayed torsos and pitched them aside with gleeful contempt.

Er Shi Huangdi was not one to be mocked; he raised his golden sword and yelled, *"Charge!"*

Ming Guo's response was to raise his own sword and respond with a battle cry of, *"Freedom! Freedom!"*

As the epic clash began, the two armies of the undead ran headlong toward each other, the terra-cotta minions of the Emperor against his risen murder victims.

O'Connell, tearing his sleeve, freed himself from under the ruined foundation, and he and Evy ran to take cover behind some rocks, from which they began picking off terra-cotta warriors. Under the firepower of the Russian submachine gun, the front line of red-clay warriors shattered like a row of piñatas, sans the candy.

Pleased with the weapon his son had given him, O'Connell smiled grimly, surveying the shards of scattered pottery, and said, "Welcome to the twentieth century, boys."

Elsewhere a phalanx of Foundation zombies was ramming into Yang's twentieth-century troops, who were getting their own 200 BC welcome as modern weapons fired to no avail, the ancient warriors overwhelming them with sheer numbers.

Yang was holding his own as the zombies bore down on him and, blowing off the skull of one, he saw the rest of the skeleton drop like the pile of bones it was, and the general made a useful discovery.

"Shoot for their heads!" Yang yelled to his men. *"Take off their heads!"*

His men followed orders, and machine-gun bursts and swinging bayonets did well with the undead attackers, although those who survived commandeered guns and, at first, used them as clubs, until observation of their foes taught the Foundation warriors quickly how to use these fire sticks. Possessed now with German-made machine guns that Yang had assigned to his best men, the zombies were quick studies, firing off full auto clips and decimating a wave of Yang's flesh-and-blood troops.

On the battlefield, Ming Guo's zombie warriors were throwing themselves wholesale at the terracotta enemy; many of the Foundation warriors were destroyed in the effort, but others armed themselves with the fallen swords and spears of their foe, and hand-to-hand combat broke out between clay soldiers and zombie warriors.

At an ammo dump in General Yang's camp, munitions were being shuttled to the front by couriers on Triumph motorcycles with sidecars, the latter to be piled with ammo boxes and spare rifles. Two such couriers had just mounted up and were speeding toward the front when—from either side, where they'd been hidden behind tents—Alex and Lin knifed through the air, feetfirst. Kung fu kicks took both couriers out, flipping them off their bikes, with Alex and Lin dropping down onto the empty seats to take the couriers' places.

This exchange had not gone unnoticed, but Alex

and Lin quickly throttled away, gunfire chasing but not catching them.

Alex's mother and father were not doing as well. They were out in the open now, their position having been overrun by terra-cotta infantry. O'Connell changed magazines on the Russian submachine gun and blasted the nearest warriors into dust and shards. They were retreating toward what they hoped would be sufficient cover, and Evy was blasting away with her twin automatics, as O'Connell's PPS 43 laid down general cover and created considerable destruction.

As he took one or two terra-cotta soldiers out at a time, with short bursts from the Russian weapon, O'Connell made his feelings clear: "I . . . really . . . *hate* . . . mummies!"

More warriors were roaring toward them, spears out to run the couple through, archers firing with long bows.

"I think," Evy said, "the feeling may be mutual. . . ."

O'Connell concentrated his hellfire on a line of warriors nearby, cutting them in half. A half-decapitated terra-cotta soldier kept coming, screeching at them in ancient Mandarin.

"Shut up, clayface," O'Connell said, and gave it a vicious rabbit punch and the walking statue exploded into fragments, neither walking nor a statue any longer.

All across the battlefield, the lines were engaged, a battalion of terra-cotta warriors charging forward when they heard a sound unfamiliar to their ancient ears: engine roar.

Specifically, the roar of two motorbikes, mowing through their red-clay ranks. The warriors began to close those ranks, to overwhelm the intruders, but Alex unpinned a grenade and lobbed it to a terracotta commander.

"Catch!" he said.

Reflexively, the commander caught the ball, not sure what it was exactly. And he never was sure, as it exploded with a blast that turned him and many around him to so much reddish-brown powder, a dust cloud through which the twin motorbikes roared.

Er Shi Huangdi, astride his magnificent black steed, was plowing through the Foundation zombies, swinging his sword and taking off skulls. He was thus engaged when he spotted, on a nearby slope, a familiar female figure, just standing there waiting for him.

"Zi Yuan!"

He leaped from his saddle and strode toward the figure and in seconds stood gazing up the rise at the woman whose charms he had coveted, so many centuries ago—the woman who had cursed him and stolen everything from him, including his life.

"Zi Yuan," he repeated.

She did not bow to him; her eyes were as hard as they were dark. She remained beautiful, though age had touched her, if lightly.

She said, *"It is time to finish what we started."*

So on the edge of the great battle, these two venerable opponents sought their own great battle, racing toward each other with swords drawn. When those swords clashed, sparks rose, thanks to the strength of this Emperor, who was not a towering figure for all his presence, and this slender woman, who should not have had the power to stand up against such a man.

But she did, matching him stroke for stroke, blow for blow, until finally they paused, each catching breath.

Er Shi Huangdi said, *"Ming Guo taught you well."*

"No," Zi Yuan said. *"I taught myself over the ages . . . preparing for this moment."*

The sword battle continued, each duelist inserting martial-arts moves, leaps, kicks, into the fray, arms and legs a blur, the flashing blades making music, and then the Emperor finally managed to slice across Zi Yuan's arm.

And she began to bleed.

The Emperor reared back and smiled. *"So . . . you are no longer immortal."*

Zi Yuan's reply was to charge him in a violent flurry. Again he met her every thrust with a parry and she his, though he did not notice when her eyes flicked to the dragon dagger on his belt.

As they faced each other, clenched hilt to hilt, Er Shi Huangdi smiled viciously. *"Know that after I kill you, I will enslave your daughter. . . . She will be my new concubine."*

They continued to trade blows until, finally, summoning all of his power, Er Shi Huangdi knocked the sword from Zi Yuan's grasp.

She stood before him, unarmed. *"You could have used mastery of the elements over me, Er Shi Huangdi. Why did you not?"*

"You could have used your powers of sorcery against me, Zi Yuan? Why did you not?"

Neither could answer.

Then, through a smile of serene confidence, Zi Yuan said, *"You will never win."*

He held out the sword, ready to run her through. *"I already have."*

But she surprised him one last time, plunging herself onto his sword, letting it enter her deep and through and through, collapsing onto him.

"At last," he said, *"we embrace."*

Then he yanked the sword from the woman and she dropped to her knees and, as he turned and strode back into battle, fell onto her side. Er Shi Huangdi did not see the dragon dagger, now in the dying Zi Yuan's grasp.

Near a turret along the Great Wall, a gaggle of terracotta warriors had cornered Rick and Evy O'Connell. His PPS 43 clicked empty, and so did both her automatics.

He glanced at her. "Next time I say we've been in tougher scrapes than this? *This* is the scrape I'm talkin' about."

He snatched up two swords courtesy of fallen terra-cotta warriors and tossed one to her. Side by side, just as they'd lived and loved, the O'Connells prepared to make their last stand.

Back-to-back now, Evy said, "No regrets, darling."

"No regrets," he said.

And as coordinated as Fred and Ginger, they each decapitated a terra-cotta warrior, red-brown heads flying, smacking together to pulverize—just a little sample of what the O'Connells were capable of.

But more red-clay warriors were closing in.

·⟪ 11 ⟫·

To Pierce the Heart of Evil

The terra-cotta warriors closed in on Rick and Evy
O'Connell, who were out of ammo, and out of
time . . . or nearly out of time, because with death
drawing near, the couple gaped in amazement and relief as the approaching red-clay soldiers were suddenly
shattered by strafing thirty-millimeter cannon fire.

A squadron in the sky, put together in haste by
their compatriot Maddog Maguire, was rolling into
action, laying down hellacious fire on the troops below. A bulky Bristol Beaufighter and two single-
engine, single-seater fighters, P-40s, were currently
cutting the Emperor's lines to ribbons.

Up in Maguire's old gray monster, Jonathan was
manning a .30-mm out the side door, yelling, "Die!
You bleeding mummy bastards . . . *die!*"

Hyper with his own heroism, Jonathan grinned over at Maguire, who looked back from the controls. "Don't you just love the smell of burning terra-cotta in the morning!"

Below, the Emperor was raising a fist to shake at the sky and roaring in rage as the planes streaked by, strafing across the battlefield. He could not allow the tide to turn and, Zi Yuan forgotten, he summoned his mastery over the elements to shape-shift . . .

. . . *becoming a giant, lionlike Foo dog, ten feet to its withers.*

The great beast the Emperor had become howled with vengeful rage and charged on all fours, crushing terra-cotta soldiers and Foundation zombies alike under its massive clawed paws. When a low-flying P-40 strafed the Foo dog's path, the beast leaped onto the back of the plane and used the machine's own weight to help drag it toward the earth. Like a man on a hang glider, the Foo dog touched down, but the plane wasn't so lucky, smashing to bits, its propellers chewing up zombie warriors like a ghoulish gardening tool.

Elsewhere, the O'Connells and their empty weapons were facing a handful of terra-cotta survivors from the strafing attack. But those attackers were chopped up by machine-gun fire from the ground, not the air, as Alex and Lin came skidding up on motorbikes.

Alex asked his parents, "You two okay?"

"Oh, yeah," his father said, wide-eyed. "No problem."

Evy blew tendrils of hair from her smudged face. "We had it utterly under control—can't you tell? You wouldn't happen to have any spare bullets?"

Their son tossed each parent a machine gun from his sidecar.

Alex grinned at his dad. "You wouldn't care to drive, would you? I'd just as soon shoot."

"Deal," O'Connell said, and sat on the front of the bike, his son climbing aboard behind him. Evy climbed on in back of Lin, but before they could roar off, they all saw the latest manifestation of the Emperor's powers—the giant Foo dog was bounding across the landscape, crushing zombie warriors underfoot as he made for the Great Wall.

Alex swore and said, "Doesn't that clown ever run out of tricks? Where the bloody hell's he *going*?"

"To the chamber," Lin said, "under the Wall."

Evelyn's eyes widened. "My God—if Er Shi Huangdi reaches that altar, he could reverse Zi Yuan's spell, and destroy the Foundation Army!"

O'Connell revved the bike. "So, then, why don't we *stop* his evil ass. . . ."

"Wait!"

It was Lin.

"My mother . . ."

They turned to where Lin was pointing and saw Zi Yuan across the field from them, crawling toward a ruined section of the Great Wall.

"*Mother—no!* She's *hurt* . . ."

Zi Yuan, dragging herself along, did not seem to hear.

"Come on," O'Connell said, and he and Alex rode over to her, with Lin and Evy just behind.

They arrived just as the sorceress had crept inside a collapsed section of stone, to shield herself from the battle. Lin jumped off her bike and ran to her fallen mother and knelt beside her.

With a faint smile, Zi Yuan noted her daughter's presence, and withdrew the dragon dagger from under her bloodstained robes.

In English, keeping no secrets from their friends, Zi Yuan said to Lin, "Take the dagger. Pierce the heart of evil. We *must* fight on. . . . You, my daughter, who I love more than life . . . *you* must fight on. . . ."

Lin accepted the dagger, but set it aside when Zi Yuan seemed to collapse into herself, and daughter took mother into her arms as the lovely sorceress left the temporal plain.

Evy picked up the magic weapon and handed it to her husband.

"You heard," she said to the O'Connell men. "Through the *heart*."

Neither O'Connell nor Alex nodded; their steely gazes were response enough.

O'Connell said, "Lin—I'm sorry. But I need you to direct us to the entrance to the Foundation Chamber."

Still at her mother's side, she looked up, nodded, and did as she was asked.

Then O'Connell and Alex mounted the bike, father in front, son behind, and sped off, leaving Evy to stay with the mourning Lin and her late mother.

The secret entrance to the Foundation Chamber was no secret to Er Shi Huangdi, who padded down the tunnel as a giant Foo dog and then swiftly transformed to his human, black-armored state, elegant and regal as ever.

The Emperor passed the astrolabe, at one end of the chamber, which began to revolve as he went by; troughs of coal oil ignited, lighting the huge chamber and, spontaneously, braziers atop stone dragon heads burst with flame as if in welcome to their long-absent ruler, lighting the walkway to the foot of the altar stairs. The waterwheel began to turn and an underground stream started flowing in its trough.

Er Shi Huangdi strode down the flame-lighted pathway and up the great staircase to stand before the altar, where, in one sweeping gesture, he raised all five elements—a spinning ball of fire, an orb of ice, a sphere of molten metal, a ball of mud, and another of rich-grained wood. All revolved before him, as if he were a juggler of mystical proportions, which indeed he was.

What he intended next, however, would require all of his powers, and intense concentration. He closed his eyes and began. . . .

* * *

As the Triumph raced along, heading toward the Great Wall and the chamber entrance, Alex asked his father, "So, Dad—what's the plan?"

"How about 'divide and conquer'?"

"Really?"

"What's wrong with it?"

"No offense, but that's a trifle light on details, isn't it?" .

"Well, son, I figured this time we'd use a page out of your book."

"What page is that?"

"The one that says, 'Play it by ear.' "

That made Alex smile, but then he heard machine-gun fire behind him, and alongside them, dirt was ripping up, the ground powdering under an onslaught of slugs.

"We have company!" O'Connell said.

"I noticed!"

Alex maneuvered himself around so that he was riding backward, and saw they were being tailed by a jeep with the beautiful Colonel Choi manning (so to speak) a .30-mm cannon, and Yang straddling the door, foot on the running board, driving with one hand and blasting away with the other as the little vehicle *bump-bump-bump*ed across the rough terrain.

Alex let the submachine gun rip away at them, but he was clearly outgunned. He could really use some support about now . . .

. . . and fortunately, in the sky, Uncle Jonathan was about to provide it.

Maguire had lost one plane but the other three, his own included, were crisscrossing over the battalions of terra-cotta warriors, raining destruction, machine guns pumping, turning the battlefield into a glorified skeet range.

Slugs from Yang's flesh-and-blood troops were occasionally thwacking into the sheet metal around Jonathan as he sat in the door with a great big bomb on his lap while he fired his machine gun down from his perch.

From the pilot's seat came Maguire's voice: "Remember our deal, mate! My crew gets to drink for free for the rest of our unnatural lives. . . ."

"You can *have* the bloody bar for all I care," Jonathan said. "I'm getting the hell out of China. I've seen enough of this pesthole."

"Where are you headed?"

"Somewhere, *anywhere*, with no *mummies*!"

And as casually as a paperboy delivering the morning news, Jonathan dropped the bomb out the door, just as Colonel Choi had the O'Connell bike dead in her sights, which did her no good at all as Alex's uncle's bomb scored a direct hit, the huge explosion upending the jeep and sending Yang and Choi flying.

Alex figured both of that pair *must* be dead . . . but

on the other hand, those two bad pennies had proved remarkably resilient thus far. . . .

His father was saying, "It's up here, behind these ruins. . . ."

"What is?"

"The entrance. The tunnel."

The Emperor's concentration was bearing results. On the battlefield, Foundation warriors were falling to their knees, wailing, writhing in agony. Their skeletal forms were being drawn backward toward the Great Wall, as Er Shi Huangdi exerted his all-powerful force.

Lost in his trance, the Emperor kept the elemental balls spinning before him, doing his mystical bidding, but he quickly snapped from it when those five balls—one at a time but in quick succession, *bang, bang, bang, bang, bang*—were blown away like pie plates at a shooting match.

At the bottom of the stone steps, Alex O'Connell was grinning up at the Emperor, who stood framed between dragon's-head pillars. Er Shi Huangdi glowered down with malevolent eyes at the youth in the leather jacket, who stood there defiantly, gun still smoking.

Alex, wanting there to be no mistake as to his intent, spoke to Er Shi Huangdi in ancient Mandarin: *"I dug you up, you damn demon, and now I'm going to put you back down."*

And on the rolling plain beyond the Great Wall, the Foundation Army was free of the Emperor's mystical force; and they charged forward, back into battle, once again.

Infuriated, the Emperor took a flying, somersaulting leap down the stairs, transforming in midair back into the giant Foo dog, whose crushing landing Alex barely avoided. What the boy could not avoid was a vicious swipe of the beast's muscular forelimb, which sent him flying across the chamber, past the astrolabe, where he hit the stone wall so hard, he crumpled like a boneless man, just a limp form in the back corner near the waterwheel.

Bleeding from his nose, and with cuts above his eyes, the young man seemed finished, out of the fray. . . .

But his father wasn't.

Rick O'Connell came out of nowhere to grab a sacred tripod and swing off it and launch himself at the beast, landing on its furry back in a painful mount, and once again he was on a bucking bronco, not a bronze steed this time, rather a giant Chinese lion/dog, between whose shoulder blades he plunged the dragon dagger.

The beast howled in pain and reared violently, tossing its unwanted rider off, O'Connell colliding with a burning brazier near his unconscious son, the thing collapsing in a shower of flame.

* * *

Lin led Evy via another way into the chamber, through a room of giant stone cogs that ran the bigger room's waterwheel. Guns drawn, the two women passed through the machinery-grinding subchamber, but did not see General Yang—scorched, tattered, bloody—on a platform above. However bedraggled, Yang remained dangerous, as he demonstrated by diving onto the two intruders.

Knocked to the stone floor, both Evy and Lin lost their pistols, the weapons skittering away; but Lin was immediately back on her feet, and launched herself at Yang. Evy was about to pitch in, when Colonel Choi, a scorched ghost of herself, blocked the way.

Evy half sneered. "Back for another lesson?"

And, just as they had done at the Shanghai Museum when this adventure was just beginning, Evy and Choi fell into martial-arts stances.

Rick O'Connell picked himself up, but noticed his fallen boy, and leaned to gently shake him. "Alex! *Alex!*"

His son did not stir.

His son looked dead.

Across the chamber, down the long pathway between burning oil fires that led to the altar stairway, the Emperor transformed from Foo dog to Er Shi Huangdi and, as if dealing with a troublesome insect, removed the dagger from his back. The blade had not found his heart.

O'Connell said, "Oh, hell," as he saw the Emperor with his arm drawn back to throw the dagger.

The adventurer flew past the astrolabe to dive under the blade as it sailed in his direction but the Emperor had anticipated this, and the blade landed close to O'Connell's head, barely missing, the blade snapping near the hilt and clattering to the stone floor.

O'Connell got to his feet and stepped out into the open and faced the small yet commanding figure in ancient black armor. For a man several thousand years old, the Emperor had a boyish countenance, but for the eyes of ageless evil.

"No more tricks," O'Connell said, fueled by a father's rage. "Fight like a man!"

The language barrier did not prevent the Emperor from understanding this challenge.

And Er Shi Huangdi was nothing if not proud. There would be no shape-shifting, no use of his mastery over the elements—a man from two centuries before the birth of Christ would meet another from the twentieth century AD, in hand-to-hand, warrior-to-warrior combat.

They charged at each other.

Meeting halfway down the path to the altar stairs, the opponents brought wildly differing styles to the fight—the skillful, even balletic martial arts of the Emperor against the hard-earned if utilitarian technique of the soldier of fortune.

At first O'Connell's size advantage seemed to

hold sway, but soon Er Shi Huangdi's lightning-fast skills overcame that advantage, and the first hard wave of punishment was taken by O'Connell.

In the waterwheel's machinery room, Evy was similarly taking a beating, tumbling down the steps and smacking against a giant cog. Choi dove on top of Evy and began to choke her.

Lin, engaged in her own martial-arts duel with Yang, saw Evy's predicament but could not tear away, the general's blistering assault demanding all of her attention.

Fighting for breath, Evy reached behind her, latched on to a moving cog and was lifted along with her opponent. As they rose, Choi's grip was threatened, then finally the colonel had to let loose, and dropped as Evy continued to be lifted by the massive machinery.

And when Choi hit the floor, Lin was able to spare a hooking kick that caught the colonel in the face, perhaps providing the makings of another scar. Evy watched, relieved, as Choi fell to the floor, down for the count.

Then she dropped to the stone floor to join Lin against General Yang.

In the Foundation Chamber, Alex came around to see his father in the midst of mano a mano with the Emperor. Why Er Shi Huangdi was not resorting to magic was beyond Alex, but his father seemed to be doing all right, in a brutal match between kung fu blows and hard-knuckled brawling.

As he pushed himself up, Alex noticed his own blood trailing down into the wide gutter fed by the underground stream under the floor; trenches of water passed on either side of the fire-lighted pathway to the altar, flowing on by, possibly coming up around behind the altar.

A tiny smile formed at the same time as a big idea. . . .

O'Connell had gained the upper hand, and now had his hands around the Emperor's throat while kneeing the bastard in the chest, again and again, with a viciousness born from the assumption his son had not survived.

Overpowered, the Emperor changed the rules—and himself back into terra-cotta. Immediately, O'Connell's repeated blows served to pulverize the hard clay. Finally he hurled the terra-cotta torso into the astrolabe, and the Emperor smashed into thousands of shards.

O'Connell, breathing hard, bleeding here and there, stumbled toward the waterwheel, and the corner where he'd left Alex. He was not aware that, behind him, those clay shards were reassembling and turning to flesh. . . .

But when O'Connell reached the corner where Alex had lain, the boy was gone.

"Alex!" he called.

And then the father noticed something: at his feet

was the broken hilt of the dragon dagger and something else—a "plus" sign, written in blood. . . .

Divide, he thought, *and conquer.*

As he turned, O'Connell saw Alex, in a dead man's float, in the water gutter heading for the altar. And he understood what his son had in mind. This realization came to him just half a second before a big fireball was flung at him.

The ball of flame knocked him off his feet and propelled him over the astrolabe, setting him ablaze.

Nonchalantly, O'Connell's screams meaning nothing to him, Er Shi Huangdi turned and headed down the pathway to the stairs and the altar, where he would finish what he'd begun, and reclaim the souls of those sorry slaves who'd rebelled against him today.

In the cog room, General Yang suddenly leaped away from the two women; it seemed at first a strange capitulation, but Evy realized the man had spotted her fallen revolver, down underneath the cogs.

She ran to stop him, but in one swift move, Yang caught her legs in his own scissored ones, and sent her crashing down, hard. Then he jammed the fallen Evy in the neck, with his boot heel, while retrieving the lost revolver by kicking it with his other foot, up near his grasp.

Lin moved quickly in, just in time for Yang to sweep the pistol snout in her face.

Yang said, "So—you would prefer to die first?"

But it was Evy who responded, "After *you* . . ."

And she straight-legged her foot into his groin with an impact that created instant agony, distracting him while Lin kicked the gun from his fingers, the weapon going off harmlessly.

Evy, now able to slip from Yang's grip, got to her feet to join Lin in simultaneous kicks to the general's chest that sent him tumbling back against the grinding cogs.

His jacket caught in their gears, and then dragged him along for the ride into its giant, gnashing teeth.

Choi was rising from the floor to stare in horror as Yang futilely tried to pull himself free.

In Mandarin, the lovely scarred colonel cried out, *"No, my love! No . . ."*

And Evy and Lin became spectators, watching Choi race to Yang's aid. Neither had guessed that the general and the colonel were an item, but indeed they were, as was evident by what followed.

Choi grabbed Yang's arm and tried to wrench him free, coming dangerously close to the giant gears herself.

He protested: *"Let go!"*

But she responded with, *"Never!"*

And an instant later he was sucked deep into the mechanism, in a horrible symphony of crunch and splash. Still holding on to her lover's hand, Choi gave the other two women a brief, serene smile before she herself was similarly sucked into those crushing cogs.

Evy and Lin stood in silence, the bizarre sacrifice somehow a moving one to both women.

"I would do the same for Rick," Evy admitted.

"And I," Lin said, "for your son."

In the midst of the struggle, and the horror, the two women had reached a new understanding.

The Emperor stood at the foot of the altar, preparing to take up where he'd been interrupted. He did not expect to be interrupted again.

But he was.

Behind him came a voice: "Is that all you got?"

And Er Shi Huangdi wheeled to see a scorched, dripping-wet Rick O'Connell, the hilt of the broken dagger tight in his fist, coming up the last few steps to the altar platform.

On what he knew was a likely suicide mission, O'Connell charged the Emperor, who smiled as he stepped forward to meet this pitiful challenge.

The Emperor, his back to the altar now, could not see Alex O'Connell—hidden on the other side, and also dripping wet—come up and over with the blade grasped in both hands, launching himself, his body like a bow ready to release an arrow.

The *whoosh* of air bid the Emperor turn his head, but too late, Alex slamming the blade into the man's back, while his father's momentum drove the hilt against the black breastplate and the blade, like a magnet seeking metal, shot through the even blacker heart.

And when O'Connell pulled the hilt back, he was amazed to see the blade magically reattached.

Agape, stunned in pain and in full realization of his doom, Er Shi Huangdi fell to his knees, as if in prayer, at the feet of Rick O'Connell . . .

. . . who leaned in close to say through lips peeled back over a ghastly grin: "Give my regards to Imhotep."

Then O'Connell had to step back, because the most amazing transformation of all was beginning. Evy and Lin were below now, having come in from the cog room just in time to share in the fantastic, horrific results of the father and son's heroism.

Liquid was pouring from the Emperor's chest wound; not blood, no, but red-hot magma, burning away the battle armor and the flesh beneath it, lava fountaining forth as if all of Er Shi Huangdi's sins were bubbling out. His heart, withering under the on-slaught, was pounding like a battle drum that all in the chamber could hear.

"When Er Shi Huangdi was cursed," Lin somberly said to Evy, "he burned from the outside in. Now he burns from the inside out."

And he was: his eyeballs were cooking white, right up to the moment when the magma exploded.

The O'Connell men were already halfway down the steps, but they looked back like Lot's wife and saw their powerful foe reduced to writhing on the platform, being absorbed into a pool of molten clay.

By the time father and son were at the bottom of that stairway, Er Shi Huangdi was just a smoking indentation on the platform's floor, vaguely suggesting a once human form.

And on the battlefield, the terra-cotta warriors, who had seemed on the verge of victory against their skeletal foes, began to crack like pots dropped onto tile floors—their weapons, their armor, their steeds, everything crazed with fissures before they toppled to the earth and became just so much more desert dust, if red-tinged . . . leaving the Foundation soldiers to stand in motionless amazement at their unexpected victory.

When the O'Connells and Lin dashed into the daylight, one more amazing sight awaited them in this day of amazing sights: the Foundation soldiers were cheering in elation as the traces of their foes were blown away on the wind.

Then, from their ravaged ranks stepped their general—the great Ming Guo.

Lin stared at the decayed, dignified figure and said, "Father?"

He seemed to smile across the battlefield at her, but father and daughter were not destined to share a moment, because the sky cracked open and a magnificent shaft of bright light shone down. Desiccated flesh and bone disintegrated, and the soldiers who'd fought so bravely this day, the slaves who'd suffered in Er Shi Huangdi's hellish servitude so long, became motes of dust in the brightest of light.

A cloud passed over and the bright shaft of light was gone and, so, were the brave men that Rick O'Connell had rakishly dubbed "zombie good guys."

"At last," Lin said, "they have achieved their goal."

Alex looked at her. "Their goal?"

She turned to him with moist eyes. "They are free."

Then, but for a gentle wind, the battlefield fell silent.

·⟨ 12 ⟩·

The Next Adventure

Shanghai's hottest nitery, Imhotep's, was packed with high-class tourist trade in honor of its new owner, Seamus "Maddog" Maguire, who had also inherited Jonathan Carnahan's blue brocade tuxedo. The Egyptian trappings remained the same, and the band was, as usual, first-rate, right now going through a medley of Tommy Dorsey tunes. As the proprietor passed along the edge of the dance floor, he noted two couples dancing slow and way off tempo, but all Maddog did was smile. He understood.

These two couples were Rick and Evy O'Connell, and Alex O'Connell and a young woman known only as Lin, a striking lass to Maguire's eyes, though truth be told he wasn't sure she was old enough to be served alcoholic beverages, even in a city as freewheeling as Shanghai.

But Maddog was in no mood to cause the O'Connell party trouble; they'd had their share of that lately. Let them celebrate, like he was.

Alex was gazing dreamily into Lin's dark, lovely, mysterious eyes. "You dance swell for an older woman," he said.

"You're all right," she said, melodically, "for a youngster. Anyway, somebody me told me something once."

"What's that?"

"Stop living on the sidelines. You might miss out. And something else . . ."

"Yes?"

"You can live a lifetime in just one look."

"Hmm. Sounds like a very smart bloke."

Her smile was as mysterious and lovely as her eyes. "Wise beyond his years . . ."

And they kissed, still way off tempo and yet in perfect time with each other.

Rick O'Connell was giving his wife one of those lifetime's worth of loving looks. "So how about it? You ready to support me again?"

A wonderful smile blossomed on Evy's beautiful face. "How's that?"

"I think I've fixed you up with enough research so you can get back to the typewriter. Don't you figure Dash and Scarlet have their next adventure ready to go?"

"Maybe I don't want write about such things anymore."

"Oh?"

"Why write about it when you can live it. . . . Anyway, can we agree that retirement is not our style?"

"Oh yes. Though I wouldn't mind putting mummies behind us."

Her smile turned surprisingly wistful. "But, darling, you must admit there's something terribly romantic about vanquishing the undead."

"True. And even more romantic doing it with you."

Her smile was shape-shifting into a pucker. "Kiss me, why don't you?"

"You don't have to ask me twice, Mrs. O'Connell. . . ."

They were kissing as Jonathan Carnahan, in rather nondescript traveling attire, suitcase in hand, was heading toward the stairs that led up to the street. Maguire crossed to him.

Jonathan nodded toward the dance floor. "Don't tell them I'm leaving. I am simply rotten at good-byes."

"I get you, mate. But they're gonna miss you. Me, too, truth be told."

The two men shook hands warmly.

Maguire put his hands on the hips of Jonathan's former tuxedo. "Where are you off to, old son?"

"South America beckons. Tropical beaches and a sea of suntanned beauties. And . . ." He leaned in to whisper. ". . . boundless opportunities to seek one's

245

fortune. Fame, I've had my fill of. Tell you what, Mr. Maguire—I'll drop you a telegram when I arrive."

Within moments, Jonathan was stepping into a taxi, telling the driver, "Airport, please, and step on it. I'm off to a place where they've never *heard* of mummies."

The Chinese driver stared at him blankly.

Jonathan sighed. "You have no idea what I'm saying, do you? I'd be better off talking to a yeti or perhaps a yak. Oh well." And he struggled to get his point across in wretched Mandarin.

Finally the taxi pulled into busy traffic on the neon-lined street, Jonathan feeling a pang leaving the O'Connells behind, but honestly not seeing any reason why they might ever find an excuse to come visit him in Peru.

He was of course unaware that, before too very long, while digging a well, a Chinese farmer in the town of Xi'an would discover the tomb of the terra-cotta warriors, which would come to be considered one of the greatest wonders of the ancient world. How they returned to their terra-cotta state after the great battle near the colossus of Er Shi Huangdi would be a mystery that Rick and Evy O'Connell, and their son, Alex, would one day come to discuss.

The O'Connells would also discuss the strange coincidence that almost simultaneously, Incan mummies were found in the mountains of Peru.

But that is another story.

Author's Note

Having written the tie-in novels based on the screenplays for both *The Mummy* (1999) and *The Mummy Returns* (2001), I was delighted to be asked back to chart the O'Connells' third adventure. My thanks to Stephen Sommers, the creator of the characters and the concept, and to screenwriters Alfred Gough and Miles Millar, who have continued the saga so well.

I am particularly grateful to Cindy Chang of Universal Studios, who was extremely helpful, getting me various drafts of the screenplay as well as visual reference that made the process smooth and enjoyable. Readers of movie tie-ins are often unaware that these books have to be written from the screenplays only, with no access to the film itself (which is often being shot at the same time the novel is being written). With a story as visually driven as this one, reference materials are key to making the novel compatible with the film, and I thank Cindy for her stellar support.

I would also like to thank and acknowledge editors Tom Colgan and Kristen Weber; my friend and agent, Dominick Abel; and my wife (and live-in editor), Barbara Collins, the Evy to my Rick, as well as Nate Collins, our Alex, who helped me figure out a key action scene.

About the Author

MAX ALLAN COLLINS was hailed in 2004 by *Publishers Weekly* as "a new breed of writer." A frequent Mystery Writers of America Edgar® Award nominee, he has earned an unprecedented fourteen Private Eye Writers of America Shamus nominations for his historical thrillers, winning for *True Detective* and *Stolen Away*.

His graphic novel *Road to Perdition* is the basis of the Academy Award–winning film starring Tom Hanks and directed by Sam Mendes. His comics credits include the syndicated strip *Dick Tracy*; his own *Ms. Tree*; *Batman*; and *CSI: Crime Scene Investigation*, for which he has also written video games and a *USA Today*–bestselling series of novels.

An independent filmmaker in the Midwest, he has

written and directed such features as the Lifetime movie *Mommy* and the recent DVD release, *Eliot Ness: An Untouchable Life.* His produced screenplays include the HBO World Premiere *The Expert* and the current *The Last Lullaby*, based on his acclaimed novel *The Last Quarry*.

His other credits include film criticism, short fiction, songwriting, trading-card sets, and movie/TV tie-in novels, among them the international bestsellers *Saving Private Ryan*, *Air Force One*, and the Scribe Award–winning *American Gangster*.

Collins lives in Muscatine, Iowa, with his wife, writer Barbara Collins.